The heel on one of the ridiculously high heels she was wearing had snapped off.

"Having a bad morning?"

The woman looked up in annoyance, strands of dark wet hair falling across her face.

"You could say that. I don't suppose you have a shoe repair place in this town?"

Nate shook his head as he approached her. "Nope. But hand it over. I'll see what I can do."

A perfectly shaped brow arched high. "Why? Are you going to cobble them back together with..." She gestured around widely. "Maybe some staples or screws?"

"Technically, what you just described is the definition of cobbling, so yeah."

Something about this soaking-wet woman amused Nate. He couldn't help admiring this woman's ability to hold on to her superiority while looking like she accidentally went to a water park instead of the business meeting she was dressed for. To be honest, he also admired the figure that red suit was clinging to as it dripped water on his floor.

He held out his hand. "I'm Nate Thomas."

She let out an irritated sigh. "Brittany Doyle." She slid her long, slender hand into his and gripped it with surprising strength. He held it for just a half second longer than necessary before shaking off the odd current of interest she invoked in him. He turned his hand palm up and she dropped the broken heel into it.

Dear Reader,

Nate Thomas hates change. He's the fifth-generation owner of the hardware store in Gallant Lake, and that legacy is important to him. He wants the store *and* his hometown to stay the same as always. He's suspicious of anything that threatens that.

When Brittany Doyle shows up with her fancy clothes and take-charge attitude, Nate's skeptical. He should be, because she's there to help her boss change the town forever, quietly buying up businesses to raze them and build vacation condos. Her boss promised her a partnership if she succeeds.

She and Nate couldn't be more opposite—flannel shirts vs. designer suits. And yet...there's something sizzling between them that they can't deny. Add in a scrappy stray mutt and a foul-mouthed parrot, and life starts changing in a hurry.

Love is in the September air, but once Nate finds out the real reason Brittany came to Gallant Lake, they have to decide what their priorities truly are. Some things are worth changing for.

It's not surprising that I wrote a book all about coping with change at the same time that himself and I decided to pack up and move from North Carolina back home to upstate New York! There were times in this move when change definitely did *not* feel good, but we embraced it as a team and took turns holding each other up. Just as Nate and Brittany learn to do.

I hope you enjoy following their journey as much as I did!

Happy reading!

Jo McNally

Changing His Plans

JO McNALLY

HARLEQUIN
SPECIAL
EDITION

HARLEQUIN®
SPECIAL EDITION™

Recycling programs for this product may not exist in your area.

ISBN-13: 978-1-335-89478-6

Changing His Plans

Harlequin Enterprises ULC
22 Adelaide St. West, 40th Floor
Toronto, Ontario M5H 4E3, Canada
www.Harlequin.com

Printed in U.S.A.

Jo McNally lives in coastal North Carolina with one hundred pounds of dog and two hundred pounds of husband—her slice of the bed is very small. When she's not writing or reading romance novels (or clinging to the edge of the bed), she can often be found on the back porch sipping wine with friends while listening to great music. If the weather is absolutely perfect, Jo might join her husband on the golf course, where she tends to feel far more competitive than her actual skill level would suggest.

She likes writing stories about strong women and the men who love them. She's a true believer that love can conquer all if given just half a chance.

You can follow Jo pretty much anywhere on social media (and she'd love it if you did!), but you can start at her website, jomcnallyromance.com.

To our grandchildren as they deal brilliantly
with the biggest change of all, becoming adults.

To Courtney, Jake, Megan, Ali, Eric, John and Haley.

Chapter One

Brittany Doyle *saw* the gathering storm clouds on the horizon.

She simply deemed them not worth her attention.

Clutching her leather-clad tablet and wearing her favorite I-rule-the-world stilettos, she stood on the corner of Main and Maple in the center of Gallant Lake, New York, and smiled. It was easy to see why she'd been sent here. The waitress at the resort restaurant this morning described the town as "quaint." Quaint, schmaint—this tired old town was dying. On the way into town, she passed half a dozen For Sale signs on homes. A number of businesses in town were boarded up. She couldn't blame them for leaving. Unless they could find work at the resort, what chance did a regular person have to make a living here?

Oh, sure, there was a cute coffee shop across the street from the waterfront. A custom furniture shop. A liquor store. Dress boutique. They might be able to survive. But the buildings along the water? A closed-up gift shop. A so-called consignment store that looked more like a shady pawnshop. And an ancient hardware store that was straight out of the 1930s. She took photos and tapped away on the screen with her notes. Those places would all have to go.

An old blue pickup truck rumbled down Main Street, disturbing the early-morning quiet with its non-existent muffler. A few minutes later a sleek BMW convertible purred past her, followed by a Gallant Lake police car. The officer nodded casually in her direction as he drove by. Charming, small-town Americana. Ripe for the picking.

Located in the Catskills, Gallant Lake was only a few hours from Manhattan. There was a recently refurbished resort that was already attracting tourists. A gorgeous lake—she held up her tablet and snapped a picture of it across the way—for summer fun, and mountains all around for skiing. This town was a potential year-round gold mine. The scene on her tablet was something straight out of her top secret guilty pleasure movie—*Dirty Dancing*. Maybe because she'd read in the brochure that the Gallant Lake Resort had once been one of those grand summer resorts during the '50s. The downtown brick-and-clapboard buildings hadn't changed much since then. It definitely held a Mayberry vibe. They could use that in marketing the place.

No wonder Conrad offered a six-figure bonus if she could secure the properties they needed in just two months. Quietly, efficiently and without drama. Basically, the Quest mantra.

A distant rumble of thunder echoed through Gallant Valley, which some people would find ominous, but Brittany just smirked. *Bring it on, world.* Her co-workers didn't call her The Barracuda for nothing. That bonus was hers, and so was this Podunk town. After this deal, Conrad hinted strongly that a partner position could be waiting. There was a corner office with her name on the door, she was sure of it.

She stepped into the Gallant Brew for a cappuccino. Her expectations were low, but she was pleasantly surprised as she watched the gray-haired hippie lady behind the counter. The woman knew her way around an espresso machine. And that bright red machine was state-of-the-art. She set an insulated to-go cup near the cash register and smiled at Brittany.

"We've got fresh pastries, honey, if you're hungry this morning."

Brittany smiled politely. "No, thanks. I had breakfast at the resort."

"Oh, you're visiting, then? You'll love the resort—the Randalls have done a wonderful job bringing it back to life. You're a few weeks early for leaf-peeping. Are you here for a wedding or something?"

"No, no. I guess you could say it's business-related, but really, I'm just enjoying the area." She looked out the window, across the street to the buildings that lined the lakeshore. "I see some empty storefronts in town. It's surprising with the resort as full as it seems to be." Brittany was fishing, strictly out of habit. She already knew the names of the owners of each property on Main Street. She knew that only a handful of businesses, including this coffee shop, were doing strong business in town. The resort didn't hold visitors long enough for most businesses to survive year-round. But vacation condos and luxury lake homes? *That* would bring people to Gallant Lake who would need places to shop and dine. It might even attract some chains to the area.

She realized the woman behind the counter—her name tag read "Cathy"—hadn't answered. Instead, the woman was staring at her with a great deal of uncomfortable interest.

"What kind of business did you say you were in?"

Brittany mentally kicked herself. She should have been more careful. She shrugged and flashed a bright smile as she evaded the question. "Oh, a…a friend of mine knew I was thinking of moving to the area and recommended the resort as a base for my research. Are there any towns you'd recommend?"

Cathy relaxed and started rattling off names of

Realtors and towns and properties Brittany should consider. Brittany nodded and smiled, enjoying the delicious cappuccino. After a polite period of time, she excused herself and headed for the door. Time for more recon before she started knocking on doors.

"Oh, honey, I'd stay inside if I were you," Cathy called out. "Looks like a heck of a summer storm brewing this morning. You'll get yourself soaked."

She looked at the clouds, which were now boiling and dark. Gusts of wind had the small trees near the water dancing back and forth. There was an energy in the air that made her fingers tremble slightly on the door handle. She loved the thrill of the hunt, and this just made it more fun. Cathy-the-aging-hippie might be right about the weather. But Brittany hadn't made it this far by showing fear in the face of a challenge. She laughed over her shoulder at the woman behind the counter.

"It wouldn't dare rain on me!"

Nate Thomas put his key in the back door of Nate's Hardware at exactly 6:30 a.m. He'd been doing that for over fifteen years now. The rest of his routine was just as predictable—back lights on, coffee maker started, jacket on hook, cash box removed from safe, cover pulled from the large cage outside his office. Then Nate headed up front to unlock the shop door.

Hank the parrot ruffled his bright turquoise feathers, then screamed a string of obscenities, knowing full well it was the only time he was allowed to do so. After he ran through his impressive repertoire, the bird gave a wolf whistle, and Nate whistled back. Just another day at work.

It was Tuesday, so Nate settled at the rolltop desk in the back office to go over the books and check inventory. Because that was what he did on Tuesday mornings. His first cup of black-as-tar coffee sat on a coaster his great-grandfather had bought at the Montreal World's Fair in 1967. That would have been Nathaniel Hawthorne Thomas number three. Nate was Nathaniel number six. Unfortunately, Nathaniel number five had been more interested in the racetrack and chasing skirts than the family business.

Nate promised his grandfather he'd keep this store going, just the way it had always been. That he'd keep Gallant Lake going. Gramps saw the town when it was booming, and he'd watched its slow decline as the resort fell into disrepair in the 1970s. He kept telling Nate the town could bounce back if it was smart about it. He begged Nate to make sure the town stayed smart. He'd done his best, starting a business owners' association and working on sprucing up the waterfront.

He was determined to keep his promise, even if his mother and sister wanted him to sell out and join them in Florida. What the hell would he do in Florida? Work at some impersonal box store? No, thanks.

His roots were deep in the floorboards of the eclectic old store. This was where he belonged. He stared out the window at Gallant Lake.

The water was being whipped up by gusty winds this morning, and the color of the water matched the charcoal clouds rolling in low from the west. Looked like a sharp August storm was headed their way. Sure enough, the opposite shore was white with a downpour, and he could see the rain sweeping across the water. He never tired of watching the ever-changing view from this office. He used to sit on his grandfather's knee and listen to the stories of great blizzards, the near miss of Hurricane Hazel, the great drought in the 1930s that dropped the water level so low people walked out hundreds of feet from what should have been the shoreline. Gramps would talk about the original heyday of the Gallant Lake Resort, visible a mile or so away, when the rich and famous came to Gallant Lake by carriage and train to leave the dirty air of the city behind. Beyond the resort was the pink granite castle called Halcyon. People used to whisper that it was haunted.

He and his pals used to sneak into the old place when they were kids. It was vacant back then, and they were sure they could get the ghost to show up, but no such luck. They just saw big, empty rooms paneled in mahogany, with dusty marble floors. When its current owner threatened to demolish it, it was Nate who led the community protest that started with a few people carrying signs and ended in court, where a judge declared Halcyon a landmark that couldn't be torn down. Ironically, the owner, Blake Randall, ended up refurbishing it into a family home and moving in. Nate's relationship with Blake was still a little strained, so he'd never gotten around to asking if he and his family shared the space with a ghost.

Nate leaned back in his chair and the oak planks creaked beneath him. Too bad *this* place wasn't haunted—he could charge money for ghost tours. He took another sip of coffee and closed the ledger. The books were just barely in the black, but he was getting by. Life was good enough.

Sheets of rain slapped against the window, quickly turning the view to gray. There wouldn't be much business today if this kept up, so he may as well get to work on taking inventory. He'd just started sorting the pesticides, getting ready to put most of them away until spring, when the front door swung open with a loud bang and a string of colorful swear words spoken in a female voice. He stuck his head around the corner of the fasteners aisle just in time to see a tall brunette stagger into the revolving seed display. Some of the packets went flying, but she managed to steady the display before the whole thing toppled. He took in what probably had been a very nice silk blouse and tailored trouser suit before she was drenched in the storm raging outside. The heel on one of the ridiculously high heels she was wearing had snapped off, explaining why she was stumbling around.

"Having a bad morning?"

The woman looked up in annoyance, strands of dark, wet hair falling across her face.

"You could say that. I don't suppose you have a shoe repair place in this town?" She looked at the bright red heel in her hand.

Nate shook his head as he approached her. "Nope. But hand it over. I'll see what I can do."

A perfectly shaped brow arched high. "Why? Are you going to cobble them back together with—" she gestured around widely "—maybe some staples or screws?"

"Technically, what you just described is the definition of cobbling, so yeah. I've got some glue that'll do the trick." He met her gaze calmly. "It'd be a lot easier to do if you'd take the shoe off. Unless you also think I'm a blacksmith?"

He was teasing her. Something about this soaking-wet woman still having so much…regal bearing… amused Nate. He wasn't usually a fan of the pearl-clutching country-club set who strutted through Gallant Lake on the weekends and referred to his family's hardware store as "adorable." But he couldn't help admiring this woman's ability to hold on to her superiority while looking like she accidentally went to a water park instead of the business meeting she was dressed for. To be honest, he also admired the figure that expensive red suit was clinging to as it dripped water on his floor.

He held out his hand. "I'm Nate Thomas. This is my store."

She let out an irritated sigh. "Brittany Doyle." She slid her long, slender hand into his and gripped with surprising strength. He held it for just a half second longer than necessary before shaking off the odd current of interest she invoked in him. He turned his hand palm up and she dropped the broken heel into it.

"Come on back, Brittany, and I'll see what we can do." He took a few steps before he realized she wasn't following. He turned to face her and read her expression with understanding. She had no reason to trust him. "You're right to be cautious about following strange men around, but it's ten o'clock in the morning in Gallant Lake. I'm just offering you a place to sit while you wait." A shiver ran through her. "And a towel. And a hot cup of coffee. And that's it."

Her pretty tawny-brown eyes, just a little tip-tilted at the corners, lit up at the mention of hot coffee. Her shoulders relaxed and she nodded, following him in her awkward, one-heeled gait. Nate was so busy thinking about the woman that he completely forgot about Hank.

"Hello! Hello! Hello!"

The parrot's harsh voice echoed around the shop. Brittany-in-the-red-suit let out a scream and jumped sideways, bumping into a tall stack of dog food. Nate caught the stack before it went over, then grabbed Brittany's arm to stabilize her.

"Sorry. Hank's extra loud in the morning. Here…" Nate turned to the display wall at the back of the store and grabbed a pair of orange flip-flops with bejeweled daisies on top. He handed them to Brittany, who was eyeing Hank with daggers. "I think you'd find walking a lot easier if your feet were both at the same level."

"I'd find walking a lot easier if that creature hadn't scared the shi…daylights out of me." But she snatched the sandals from his hand. "What the hell are you doing with a bird in your store? Isn't that against sanitation laws or something?"

City women.

"It's a hardware store, not a restaurant. And Hank's a very clean bird, if you don't count his language. He's a fixture here."

"Charming." That word in that tone did not sound like a compliment.

"If you'd rather walk back to your car and go somewhere else for shoe repair, I think there's a place in White Plains…" It wasn't like Nate to be rude, but he couldn't help goading this woman.

A crash of thunder answered before she could, and he noticed her mouth tightening at the sound. She didn't like the storm. She didn't like Hank. And her glare made it clear she'd leave if she could, because she didn't seem to like *him* very much, either.

But she couldn't leave in this weather, so he may as well fix her shoe. She followed him to his office, colorful flip-flops slapping on the floor, and claimed his leather chair at the desk. He went into the back room, found a beach towel and tossed it at her. Her annoyance started to fade when she wrapped it around herself like a blanket. She was probably chilled to the bone.

"What do you take in your coffee?"

"One sugar and lots of cream."

"Powdered creamer is all I have."

Her face scrunched in disgust, and Nate almost laughed.

"Again—not a restaurant. Hardware store. You want it or not?"

"Fine."

He used his mom's bright yellow mug. She hadn't been here to use it for years, but it was tradition that everyone in the family had their own mug waiting in the office. Her Majesty accepted the coffee with a mumbled, almost reluctant, "Thank you."

"Give me a minute to glue this up." He went to the bench in the other room and found his favorite bonding glue. He used it while repairing antiques. He placed a few dots far enough from the edge that they wouldn't seep through. Then the heel was pressed into place on the… He looked inside. Jimmy Choo. He'd heard of them. Expensive. He had a feeling everything about this woman was expensive.

When he walked back into the office, she was staring out at the lake. The striped towel was wrapped around her shoulders, but she'd obviously used it on her hair while he was gone. The chestnut-brown waves were drier, fluffier and had been brushed off her face. Her profile, with the backdrop of the stormy lake, was striking. A perfectly straight nose and full lips. Those large golden eyes with the upswept corners. The gold hoops hanging on her ears matched the multiple gold necklaces, and the bangles on her wrists. This woman was classy. Sharp. A real go-getter. This woman didn't belong in Nate's Hardware. She didn't belong in Gallant Lake. She turned to look at him in the doorway.

She was a grown-up version of Monica Battersby from high school. Prom queen. Valedictorian. Champion tennis player. Daddy was a doctor. Mom ran a charity foundation. Monica walked down the halls like she was walking a red carpet. She didn't waste time with anyone outside her circle of equally privileged friends. She certainly never made the time of day for Weird Nate Thomas from the hardware store.

He swallowed hard. This pretty brunette—even drenched from the rain, wrapped in a towel, wearing flip-flops—she was another Monica Battersby. She was out of his league. And still…

"Was the operation a success?"

"What?"

She held out her hand. "The shoe? Did you cobble it or not?"

"Um…yeah. Give it a little while to finish setting up before you put weight on it. You can keep the flip-flops to wear."

"I can pay for the sandals."

"I'm sure you could." His eyes gave her a once-over, taking in all her designer duds again. "I'm saying you don't have to."

She tipped her head to the side, studying him intently. Then she gave him a slow smile. The towel slid slowly off one shoulder. She wasn't Monica Battersby anymore. Now she looked more like that black-and-white poster of Sophia Loren that Gramps used to have hanging in this very office.

Gramps used to say Sophia was the kind of woman whose beauty was timeless because it was more than skin deep. Her beauty glowed from within. Gramps said Sophia wasn't a put-on. She was "The real deal, boy."

Nate had a feeling that, somewhere inside that proud, prickly attitude, Brittany Doyle might just be the real deal, too.

Chapter Two

"Conrad, you were right about this place." Brittany sat at the desk in her room at the Gallant Lake Resort, her phone pressed to her ear, her tablet propped in front of her. She slid her finger across the screen, scrolling through the photos she'd taken before the storm. "And this is the perfect time. The resort is giving people hope, but property values haven't jumped that much yet. Most of the resort's success is centered on the resort itself at this point." She looked around her room, which had clearly been updated recently. The colors were warm and contemporary. The furniture and artwork were trendy, but not so much that they'd be out of style in a year.

"I know. We've already done the research, Brittany. That's not what I sent you there for." Her boss's voice was flat. It took a lot to get Conrad Quest enthusiastic when it came to business. Maybe once she locked up the purchases he'd give her a pat on the back. Maybe.

"I realize that." She kept her voice as steady as his, while rolling her eyes wildly. "I'm just saying my observations *support* that research. No surprises that I can see at this point. The buildings on the lake side of Main Street seem to be struggling the most, which plays into our hands."

"Have you met with anyone yet?"

I've only been here one freakin' day, Conrad.

"Um…yes, of course." She'd met a tall, flannel-clad hardware store owner with thick brown hair and a beard to match. "I chatted up the lady at the coffee shop, and I met the owner of one of the properties we want—the hardware store."

"Good. And you're using your usual charm to win them over?"

That *was* the usual approach for what Conrad called his "acquisition agents." Make fake friends, get invited to all the social gatherings, win people's trust and confidence, then quietly start making purchase offers. Eventually, word always got out that people were selling, and then the company would have to pay premium prices for what they wanted. The more properties they could charm out of people before that happened, the better it was for the Quest

Properties' bottom line. If she thought about it too hard, she felt more than a twinge of *squickiness* at Quest's method. That was why she'd been working in the office these past two years, doing the research and selecting areas to target for development. It left her one step away from the face-to-face dealings.

She looked out the window at the view, with green-and-gray mountains surrounding the brilliant blue lake. The sun was beginning to go low in the sky, muting and warming the colors. This was a lovely place, and she was here to change it. She straightened. For the *better*, of course. She wasn't the villain here. Gallant Lake was in trouble, with all those boarded-up storefronts. It wasn't like Quest *stole* the first properties they bought—they paid market value. It was just that market value happened to go *up* after people learned Quest Properties was in town to build something.

"Well, it's only my first day, Conrad. But I was as charming as possible."

Except for that hardware guy. Nate. She wasn't terribly charming with *him*, but she had time to turn that around.

"Good," Conrad said. "We're on a time crunch with this one. I want that waterfront bought up as quickly as possible, and we need to keep it under the radar."

"Isn't that always the case?" Brittany was a

team player, and he knew that. "But after this one, Conrad…"

"I know." His voice was still as flat and unreadable as before. "That partnership is still on the table, and I know you want it. But first—Gallant Lake. You're my barracuda, Brittany. Make it happen."

"Got it, boss. Operation Gallant Lake Charm Offensive will begin first thing in the morning. Or maybe we should call it Operation Everyone Loves Brittany." She didn't usually joke around with Conrad. He wasn't a joking kind of guy. Sure enough, he was confused by it.

"What does that mean?"

"Just kidding—sorry." She cleared her throat, putting her all-business voice back in place. "I'm a little tired tonight and getting punchy. I'll have Gallant Lake buttoned up for you in no time."

"Well…do whatever you need to do to make sure you're ready to go in the morning. And for God's sake, don't mention my name or Quest Properties to *anyone*."

She thought of that request after the call had ended. When Quest chose an area to develop, he always had the acquisition agents come in low-key. But once word got out that they were buying up properties, he'd never cared if they knew it was him. It was part of his public persona. It was what he was known for. But with Gallant Lake, he'd set up a new corporation—Lakeshore Vacation Properties—to shield the Quest name on the

purchase offers. He'd told her it was just a precaution-
ary move, but never said what he was *precautioning*
against. In fact, Conrad had been super cagey about
Gallant Lake right from the start. And even more ur-
gent than usual.

She'd love to know why, but she had no interest in
rocking the company boat when she was this close to
that partnership. After twelve years she could almost
smell the leather in her imaginary office chair and
feel the smooth glass surface of her ultramodern desk.
The one already saved to her locked Pinterest file,
labeled "Brittany 3.0." That file was her version of a
vision board, with all the things she had determined
would be in her future. The twelve-thousand-dollar
desk was one of dozens of items on her must-have
list. Visual affirmations to the world that she would
have *arrived*.

She was Brittany 2.0 now. Good at what she did,
respected—sometimes feared—financially comfortable and fiercely tough and independent. All the
things Brittany 1.0 had never been. That girl was
gone forever, and that was a very good thing.

But right now? Brittany 2.0 was hungry. She'd
showered and changed after getting drenched in the
storm earlier. Still a suit, of course, but this was a
slightly more casual tan linen jacket and trousers
paired with a chocolate silk camisole. She pulled
her hair back into a low ponytail tied off with an
Hermès scarf, finishing the ensemble with a pair

of floral embroidered pumps with kitten heels. Her sister liked to tell her she always looked like she had a stick up her ass, but Brittany had never seen what was so terrible about looking like you cared about what you looked like. And she cared. Maybe more than she should, but this look she'd cultivated so carefully had taken her a long way in the corporate world. Her heels clicked on the gleaming lobby floor when she stepped off the elevator. She liked it when her heels clicked like that—a little drumbeat to remind her who she was now.

Eventually, she'd have to frequent the local eateries and do her reconnaissance, but tonight she just wanted a quiet meal. The resort's restaurant, Galantè, had a wall of windows overlooking the lawn that swept down to the lake. It was seven thirty on a Tuesday night, so the place was pretty quiet. She was able to get a table in the corner by the windows all to herself. One last evening of solitude before she turned on the charm and started buying up the town. There were a few men clustered together on the far side of the large oak bar, but they were talking and laughing among themselves and paying no attention to her.

The food was amazing—as pretty as it was delicious, with fronds of scallion greens standing tall above the broiled salmon, the entire plate drizzled artfully with a honey-balsamic reduction. *This* was what made Gallant Lake different from other Quest target areas. The town might be sleepy and struggling, but this resort was becoming a well-established, high-end destination. It was the boutique jewel of the Randall Resorts International stable of hotels, and the home base for the entire company. As she ate, she wondered again why Conrad wanted to compete with an enterprise like this. He usually liked to be the only game in town—he'd never been fond of battling anyone for dominance.

Brittany had realized a long time ago that Conrad preferred to be the heir apparent without question. Not because his ego was that large. It *was* large, of course. But it was also terribly fragile. After she'd learned that little secret, she'd been able to work her way up to almost-partner without looking back. As long as she could keep the boss feeling safe and secure, she had the best chance to be his right-hand woman. And someday—maybe Brittany 4.0?—she'd rule her own business empire.

There was another loud burst of laughter from those guys at the bar, timed so perfectly with her thoughts that she looked over at them, annoyed for their mocking of her. But they weren't even close to looking her way. They were huddled over someone's phone, still laughing at what was probably some juvenile online video. It was darker away from the windows, so she couldn't see their faces, but they sounded younger, and at least two of them were in dark business suits. Probably guests in town for one of the conferences at the resort. She'd seen several listed on the board in the lobby. One for New York State grape growers and winemakers—she didn't even know that was a thing. And another for some golf clinic.

She passed on dessert when the server brought the menu, knowing she'd be going to every church supper and greasy spoon in the area over the next month or so. But she *did* order a Gallant Lake Summer Fun Martini, which ended up being a dessert in a glass. The Blue Curacao and pineapple vodka obviously represented the lake. The rim of the glass was edged in dark green melted chocolate, rolled in sparkly gold sugar, to represent the mountains. A short piece of rosemary, looking like a pine branch, floated at the edge of the drink. A thin plastic skewer with a sun at the top held two pieces of soft sugar candy that looked like molded gumdrops. The lower piece was a bright orange fish, which sat under the surface of the drink. A red-and-white boat-shaped piece of candy sat right on the surface. It was a kitschy homage to the Catskills lake right outside the windows.

Brittany held the glass up and snapped a photo of it with the lake in the background. She couldn't post it on social media or anything, because no one was supposed to know where Quest Properties' top barracuda was working at the moment. But there was one person who could not only be trusted with the secret, but who would also *adore* the image. She smiled as the text whizzed off to her sister. Bubbles popped up almost immediately.

OMG! Is that a LAKE in a martini glass in front of an actual LAKE? R U vacationing?

Brittany smiled and typed a response.

I'm working, but enjoying the view—and the drink.

Actually, she hadn't tried the drink yet. She took a quick sip to avoid going to hell for lying to Eloise. It had a sharp citrus flavor, tempered with the faint earthiness of the rosemary sprig. Just like her meal, it was both pretty and delicious. No wonder this resort was so popular. Her phone pinged with a response.

Let me guess…drinking alone? You work too much. When are you coming to visit?

She cringed. She should have known the conversation would circle to this. She just hadn't expected it right off the bat.

Gotta make money, El. Once I get that partnership, I'll have more time to spend with you.

Was there any chance of Ellie buying that? She watched the bubbles wavering on her screen.

Really? Is one of the job perks a Dr. Who super-power that bends time and creates more hours a day than you have now? Cuz we both know you'd use it to work more.

She took another sip of her drink, scowling at the screen. Leave it to her little sis to lay the truth out in a few pointed questions she already knew the answers to.

Give me a break. You know why I'm doing this. Lectures were always Mom's thing, not yours.

No bubbles. She held her breath until they mercifully popped up again.

I love you, Britt-Britt. It's not your job to take care of me. But fine. Does the drink taste as tacky as it looks? Is that candy on the skewer? My teeth hurt just thinking about it.

Brittany's shoulders relaxed, and she answered that she was a little afraid to try the candy. She chatted with her sister for a few minutes and felt the weight of the traveling and lack of sleep falling away. Talking with Ellie always helped Brittany center herself. Ellie kept her grounded. Kept things real. Gave her a touchstone that reminded her of how far they'd come together. But eventually, Ellie had to get back to her studies at the university hospital. She'd graduate the following spring as a full-fledged physician assistant. So they said goodbye the same way they had for years—by sending kissing GIFs. The sillier, the better. Britt sent one of two otters smooching, and Ellie sent an old black-and-white movie clip of two 1920s flapper girls rubbing cheeks and air-kissing.

She was still smiling when she signed the bill to be charged to her room, adding a large, but not outrageous, tip. It was a force of habit after all these years—always be seen as generous, but not so much so that it will raise attention or suspicion. She was getting tired of always being so calculated. But Ellie's school bills were high, and her insulin was an added burden Brittany had vowed to handle. She asked the server if she could take the drink out to the darkening veranda outside the wall of windows, and the woman smiled and said, "Of course."

The sun was behind the mountains now, but the sky still glowed in bright shades of melon and pink. It was warm and humid, and the low hum in the air told her that bloodsucking insects would probably be chasing her inside before too long. She leaned her arms on the stone railing and sipped from her drink, slowly rotating the glass to get all the sugar-coated chocolate off the rim. This was one last moment of indulgence before getting into working mode tomorrow morning, and she was going to make the most of it.

"Of all the gin joints in the world…" A familiar low voice paraphrased Bogart behind her. "You had to walk onto this veranda."

Nate Thomas. Who owned a piece of property she needed. She put on her I-love-Gallant-Lake sunny smile before turning to face him. But for some reason she had a hard time sticking to the script with this guy. There was something about his perpetually amused expression that got under her skin, just as it had earlier. Maybe because he seemed so terribly amused by *her*.

He was still wearing the same faded plaid shirt and well-worn jeans he'd had on that morning, which should have seemed out of place at an elegant resort like this. But somehow, the man wore them like a second skin, making him look like he was very sure he belonged.

"Fancy meeting you here." She made a point to look at his attire. "Are you here to cobble more shoes? Or maybe mow the lawn?"

He chuckled, rubbing his dark stubble with one hand. His other held a bottle of domestic beer. "I don't know where *you're* from, Miss Doyle, but around here, this attire is universally accepted." He gestured toward her. "You, on the other hand, look painfully overdressed."

"There's nothing painful about it, *Mr.* Thomas." She straightened her shoulders and tried to find that charming smile again. Somehow, she suspected it looked more like a grimace. "I'm quite comfortable. What brings you to the resort this evening?" She took another sip of her blue martini, hoping it wasn't leaving her with blue lips and tongue. She was going for cool and classy here, not tipsy teenager.

"Drinks with friends. You're staying here?"

"For a few days. I have a vacation rental house lined up, but it won't be ready until Sunday." The online vacation site had described it as an "adorable one-bedroom cottage on the water with lots of vintage charm." Brittany didn't care about vintage anything, but the photos made it look clean and it wasn't far from the center of town. It had Wi-Fi. And privacy. From the website map, it was located farther out on a peninsula than the other adorable cottages the owner was renting. She could have phone calls with Conrad and talk to property owners about selling without nosy neighbors around.

"How long are you staying in town?"

A small red flag went up. "You're asking a lot of questions for a cobbler."

He laughed, and his tanned face creased into a road map of deep lines, especially around his dark eyes. This was a man who spent a lot of time outdoors. He took a drink of his beer before replying.

"I'm going to hazard a guess that you don't spend a lot of time in small towns. Small-town people are just naturally…curious."

"You mean nosy?"

He lifted one shoulder. "I prefer curious. Or maybe just call it friendly."

It was true that the only time she'd intentionally spent in any town outside Tampa was for business. To turn them into not-small-towns after Conrad built whatever he was going to build there—resorts, condos, housing developments. She needed to remember that she wanted Nate's building, which meant she shouldn't antagonize him.

"Point taken." She tipped her head, refusing to apologize out loud. Apologizing was never good for negotiating, and sooner or later she'd be negotiating with this guy. "I'm a city girl through and through." He raised a brow in an unspoken question, and she answered. "Tampa. And to answer your other question, I'll be staying here for a month or so. I've been thinking about relocating to the Northeast, so I guess you could say I'm town-shopping. Checking out a few areas before I decide." It was the story she used most often when doing advance acquisitions. People loved to tell her everything about their town, good and bad, when they thought she wanted to be one of them.

"That's a big move, from Tampa to here." He looked out at the lake, turning silver as the sunset faded into night. "I know a couple guys who've done the downsizing thing to Gallant Lake, though. One from LA and one from Boston. They made it work, but they stayed here for love, so they were motivated."

What would *that* be like, moving for real to a place like Gallant Lake? For that matter, what would doing anything "for love" be like? She lifted her glass to her lips, shoving that thought aside as she drained the last of the blue concoction.

"Ah, I see you've met the latest Gallant Lake-in-a-glass cocktail." Nate's mouth slid into a slanted smile. "They hired a new bartender last year, and she does a new martini for every season."

Brittany picked up the skewer and slid the candy fish into her mouth. The sugary candy soaked by the tart alcohol was surprisingly good.

"I give her an A for originality *and* execution." She slid the little boat down the skewer with her teeth and ate it, flashing Nate a bright smile. "And that signals the end of my first full day in Gallant Lake, with Nate Thomas at both ends of it. Thanks for fixing my shoe, by the way. Maybe I'll stop by again sometime." She brushed past him, feeling off her game again. Nate had a knack for making her very aware that she was forcing her smiles and small talk, and it irritated her. She really did need to get some sleep so she could regain her focus. "Good night."

Chapter Three

Nate watched Brittany walk across the veranda, now lit up softly with overhead strings of tiny fairy lights. When he'd seen her out here on his way back to join his friends at the bar, he figured it was a good time to ask a few questions. The resort certainly attracted its share of low-to-mid-level celebrities and wealthy clients, but those people generally stayed right here on the property. If they did wander into town, it was only to shop at the Five and Design boutique, owned by his friend's wife, Melanie. That made sense, since Mel had once been among the golden people herself as a former supermodel. Sometimes they went to the coffee shop owned by Nora Peyton, wife of another friend of Nate's. And once in a great while the upper-crust tourists would wander into his hardware store to exclaim how *quaint* it was.

They were far more likely to buy one of the antique metal signs he had hanging from the rafters than to buy actual hardware. One guy bought a whole collection of train memorabilia last month. Nate had bought a box sight unseen at an auction and found it was full of L&O toys and gadgets. He'd made a nice penny on *that* sale.

So it wasn't completely unheard of that this uptight woman draped in gold jewelry and designer clothes had come into his store, even if just to escape the downpour. But there was something…off…about Brittany Doyle. He couldn't put his finger on it, but she didn't act like a tourist. He didn't buy her story about looking for a place to live, either. Gallant Lake wasn't on any fancy list of America's Best Places to Live. It had never fully recovered from a drop in resort business back in the '70s and '80s, his family's business included. The new owners of the resort, Blake and Amanda Randall, had been working hard to put the place back on the map, but the idea that a beautiful single woman with lots of cash and expensive taste would *choose* to live here… Nope. Didn't make sense to him.

He'd intended to ask more questions, even though she'd called him out on it. But when she put her coral-colored lips around that candy boat on the skewer and slid it down and into her mouth… Well, his questions went straight out of his head. Along with his voice. He'd just stood there as she ate that damn boat, said good-night and left. Without him saying a word.

"There you are!" Asher Peyton came outside, followed by Nick West. "We thought you got lost." He looked toward the French doors Brittany had just escaped through. "Then we saw you talking to a pretty lady out here. Who was she?"

"A guest here. She came into the store this morning with a broken heel."

Asher's forehead rose. "So she went to the hardware store for what…nails? I mean, you *have* every size nail known to construction, but…"

Asher was the reason Nate stocked half those nails. His custom furniture shop was right across the street from the hardware store, and Asher was always running over for some odd size or configuration.

"She was just running from the rain this morning. I glued her shoe together, Hank yelled at her and that was that." Except he hadn't stopped thinking about her all day.

"Until tonight. Was she thanking you for saving her, Nate?" Nick teased. "Are you her Prince Charming now?"

Brittany thought Nate asked a lot of questions, but he was no match for former cop Nick West. Now the director of security for all the Randall resorts, Nick was incessantly…curious.

"Give me a break. Did you see the woman? Do

you think *that* kind of woman would consider me any kind of prince at all?" Nate gestured down to his clothes. He wasn't one to care about stuff like fashion, but he'd felt an odd little pinch when she turned her nose up at him earlier. "I saw her out here and said hi. As you saw, she left me standing here. That's it. Now, come on…" He put one arm around Nick's shoulders and the other around Asher and started marching them back inside. "If we leave Brannigan in there by himself for too long, he'll be boring the bartender with sports trivia again."

Three days later he was still thinking about Brittany. In fact, he'd thought about her all three nights, too. He kept seeing her in her tailored clothes and fancy shoes, hair pulled back. She struck him as someone very much in control. Of her looks. Of herself. She had an energy that simmered under her skin. The type of energy that didn't scream "small town" in any way. She belonged on the crowded sidewalks of a big city, striding along as she plotted to take over the planet. She stuck out like a sore thumb in his little town. He rolled over in bed, noting the sun was barely lighting the eastern sky outside the two large windows facing the lake. This was going to be a long day.

As much as Nate liked the thick dark brew he made in his shop, he also had a secret love affair with Nora's Americano at The Gallant Brew. The coffee shop was across the street from the hardware store, next door to her husband Asher's furniture studio. Nate fed Hank, listened to the daily string of obscenities, then put his Be Right Back sign on the door. He made a beeline for Nora's place. The petite brunette laughed when he walked through the door.

"Uh-oh, someone needs an Americano!"

The cozy, brick-walled coffee shop only had a few customers at tables, including Steve and John playing their daily cribbage game. He nodded their way and walked back to the counter, anchored by the massive oak-and-glass display case he'd found for Nora in a barn sale two towns over. It was taller than she was, and round, with shelves that turned to display the baked goods. When he'd found it, the display had one broken glass panel, which curved to fit the cylindrical piece. It took him months to locate one online that would fit. Asher had refinished the display and installed the glass, giving it to Nora as an anniversary gift.

She set a bakery box on the counter. "A fresh batch of espresso is finishing up now. Let me just restock the pastries and I'll pour it for you." She opened the box and started displaying the croissants, cookies and scones. "Looking for a little extra caffeine, huh?"

"Yeah, one of those nights. I need a cup of your magic bean juice to get through the day. In fact, make it a double."

Nora grinned, tucking her chin-length hair behind her ear. "Are you ready for the business owners' meeting next week? Extending the boardwalk is on the agenda."

The boardwalk had been Nate's pet project for years. The original planners of Gallant Lake over a hundred years ago hadn't fully appreciated the value of the waterfront. The businesses on the lake side of Main Street all faced the street, with storerooms and solid walls on the back—where the view was. But Nate knew the town *did* originally have a boardwalk along the waterfront. It had fallen into disrepair decades ago and had been removed. Nate started pushing for the boardwalk when he was back in high school—designing and starting it had been his Eagle Scout project. The town board approved it, but funds always seemed to come up short to actually do it. He'd built a lot of it himself, adding a new section every year.

The plan was to connect the small parks on either end of town with the boardwalk. A few more years and he might just get there. It already spanned the area behind most of the businesses on that side, including his. But people were reluctant to invest in remodeling their shops to open onto the waterfront. He understood—business hadn't been great for decades. But now that the resort was so active, tourists *were* coming downtown more. That was why he wanted the town to apply for a state grant to finish the project and capture that opportunity before even *more* shops closed for good.

"This is the time to do it, Nora, before it's too late." He gestured out the windows toward the street. "If we can finish the boardwalk and maybe add a pier for boats and more benches for folks to sit on..."

Nora slid his double-shot Americano across the counter. "You don't have to sell me on it, Nate. We need more businesses to attract more people, but we need more people to attract new businesses. It's a vicious cycle, and we need to make a bold move like this." She poured herself a coffee, then leaned on the counter and stared out the windows. "The women's group has been talking about maybe adding some small festivals or something to bring more people. Having the boardwalk finished would be a big draw. We can't afford to lose more storefronts."

They'd already lost Stella Cortland's souvenir shop. Frank and Mary's consignment shop was struggling, and Louise DiAngelo's hair salon wasn't doing much better. Rumor had it she was ready to sell it and retire. The bakery had been closed for years. If it wasn't for his side hobby of buying and selling antiques, the hardware store may not have been able to stay open this long. It barely provided him enough income to live on after the bills were paid.

Nora startled him out of his gloomy thoughts with her next comment.

"Oh, there's Brittany. She's up and out early today."

Nate straightened and turned, expecting to see her

at the door. But no, she was across the street, talking with Stella Cortland. Stella was in her seventies and split her time between Gallant Lake in the summer and Daytona in the winter. She owned the property attached to the hardware store, but she hadn't been able to keep the souvenir shop going. It had closed for the winter two years ago and never reopened, and she hadn't found a renter yet. Nate would have loved to buy the property and knock through the connecting wall, but there was no way he could afford it. Stella pointed up near the peak of her three-story brick building, where the trim desperately needed a fresh coat of paint.

Brittany Doyle held up her fancy tablet and took a picture of the damaged trim. Nate's forehead furrowed. Why would Brittany need photos of anything here, especially chipped and rotted wood trim? She took another photo of the empty shop windows, chattering away nonstop to Stella as she did. Nate frowned, turning back to Nora.

"Wait… How do you know Brittany Doyle? She's only been here a few days."

Nora arched a single brow. "Seriously? I'm the only show in town for coffee and sweets. I get to know a lot of people. I'm more interested in how *you* know Brittany *and* how you know how long she's been here."

"Did she tell you why she's in Gallant Lake?"

"Why do you sound so suspicious? She's renting one of Vince Foster's cabins on the lake." She laughed and gestured toward the windows and the lake beyond. "We *want* people, remember?" Her smile faded when he didn't laugh with her. "What's going on?"

"I don't know. She came in the store a few days ago, and she just didn't seem…" He struggled to find the right words, since he wasn't sure himself what bothered him about her. "She didn't seem to *fit* here. I mean, look at her."

It was a warm late-August morning in a rustic resort town, and Brittany was in a long, trim dress of dark blue with matching shoes. Her hair was tucked under a wide-brimmed straw hat with a white bow. It looked more appropriate for Monte Carlo than Gallant Lake. Large sunglasses covered the top half of her face. He grimaced.

"Does that look like someone who'd want to live here? With that dramatic hat and those Hollywood sunglasses…"

Instead of agreeing, Nora narrowed her eyes at him, her mouth pressed into a firm line.

"Nathan Thomas, what is *wrong* with you? I was in Five and Design yesterday when Brittany bought that hat." Her hand rested on her hip. "You know— that place my *cousin* owns? The cousin who was an internationally famous fashion model? The one who moved to Gallant Lake from Miami and *stayed*? Why are you being so quick to judge Brittany?"

Nate pulled back in surprise, but she had a point. Melanie Lowery had come to town a few years back and settled right in, bringing high fashion to Main Street with her boutique. Then she convinced another confirmed city dweller, Shane Brannigan, to move here, too. They bought a house, got married and just had a new baby boy.

"Yeah, but…" He automatically started to defend himself, but he didn't know how to put his thoughts into words. "I mean… Okay, you're right about Mel and Shane. But there's something about Brittany Doyle…"

Nora's smile returned, and she reached over to pat his arm. "Just admit it, Nate. You don't like anyone or anything new. Change is not your friend. But this town is changing." She waved toward the other side of the street. "Hell, *you're* changing it with the boardwalk. The resort is getting more and more popular, and the town…" She pointed straight at him. "The *town* has to accept that we're going to grow and change because of it. I know your family's been here forever, but they've survived all the ups and downs so far."

"But…" He sputtered for a moment. "Why is she over there taking pictures of Stella's building?"

"How should I know? Maybe she likes historical architecture. Maybe that's something you two have in common. Why don't you go ask her, Nate?" Nora nodded at four customers coming through the door, dismissing him with one last dig. "Since you seem to be so fascinated by the woman."

Nate rolled his eyes and headed back to the hardware store. He'd been gone too long as it was. Brittany and Stella were just walking into Stella's place as he crossed the street. His eyes narrowed again. Brittany had been here four days and already knew Nora, Mel and now Stella. Making herself at home? Or something else?

It was more than unsettling that she was staying at Vince's little cabins. He drove by Walnut Point on his way home every day. He could walk there easily. It was a little too close for comfort.

"Good morning, you salty son of a…"

"Hank, *no*." Nate tapped the side of the cage with his fingers. "No swearing during the day. You know the rules."

The large bird twisted his head to the side, then gave a wolf whistle. "Handsome Hank! Handsome Hank!"

Hank *was* a handsome bird, with his brilliant turquoise feathers with sapphire tips and the orange, black and white around his face. He'd been one of Nate's father's many irresponsible purchases, bought on a whim. Or maybe won in a card game—the story had always been a bit fuzzy. But the foul-mouthed parrot had somehow managed to worm his way into Nate's heart. It wasn't the bird's fault his dad had taught him every curse word known to man.

He dropped a couple of dried banana chips in one of the plastic dishes inside the large handmade cage, and Hank snatched one right away, holding it with one foot and nibbling his way around the edges. The parrot knew he wasn't supposed to use curse words after his morning tirade, but Nate had a sneaking feeling he did it once in a while just so Nate could correct him. Then he'd say something cute and get a reward. Hank was no dummy.

"You're gonna 'handsome Hank' your way into a stew pot if you're not careful."

Hank ruffled his feathers and hollered.

"Help! Help! Help!"

No, he wasn't *really* sentient, but he *was* extremely intelligent and remembered a lot of cues. Threatening him with the words *stew pot* always got him screaming "Help!" The customers loved it, and Hank loved applause. And banana chips. Nate tossed him another and headed back to his office.

There was a stack of bills on his desk that needed to be paid. But first, he fired up the computer and checked his website. Not the one for the hardware store, but the one for Gallant Lake Picker—the side business that kept this place afloat. He'd probably be better off financially if he sold off the nails and bolts and ropes and the rest of the hardware items and filled the place with the antiques he gathered on the weekends. But he didn't have it in his heart to be the one who ended the generations-long hardware business. He'd promised his grandfather he'd keep it the same as always.

He had two offers on the vintage Halcolite lights he took out of Sally Mitchell's house last week. They weren't all that priceless or rare, but it was a complete set from the 1920s, with a large chandelier and four matching wall sconces—solid bronze with all the crystal teardrops still intact.

The first offer was laughable, but the second was close to his asking price, and the buyers were up in Lake George, so they could drive down and pick them up. Not having to box and ship them was worth dropping a few bucks off the asking price. He messaged them that they now owned a set of lights. With a little bit of money coming in, he felt better about paying bills.

He'd been at his desk for an hour or so when he heard the brass bell above the front door tinkling. Hank had it covered.

"Hello! Hell-oo! Hi! Hello!"

Nate heard a woman's voice and immediately thought of Brittany. Which was weird. Maybe Nora was right in saying he was obsessed after two brief conversations. A man's voice spoke next, and Nate walked out to greet a young couple. They were looking for rope for the small boat they'd just purchased, and he set them up with enough line, as well as fiberglass polish and vinyl conditioner for the seats.

And all the while, he wondered why Brittany

Doyle had been right next door with Stella and never stopped by his place. Yeah, Nora had a point about him being obsessed, and it was time for him to shake it off and get on with his day.

Chapter Four

Brittany had been in real estate long enough that she should have known better than to sign an agreement to rent this so-called adorable cottage. *Adorable* was always a code word for *tiny*. That it was small wasn't all that shocking—the ad said it was a one-bedroom, seven-hundred-square-foot cottage. That square footage was just…smaller…than she'd anticipated. She walked outside with her coffee and looked the place over again. This was her third morning there, and the place wasn't getting any bigger.

Cottage was just as generous as *adorable* was. This was an old square clapboard box sitting on cement block supports. The cheery green metal roof appeared recent, but the rest of the place? She took in the peeling white paint and a set of sagging steps leading to a wooden screen door painted to match the roof. There wasn't much that was cheery about the rest of it.

She had been mildly relieved at the interior. It was definitely rustic, with the gray painted wood-plank flooring and a kitchenette straight out of the '50s with its tiny refrigerator and gold-flecked white vinyl counters. But it all seemed clean, and the sofa and easy chair had bright yellow slipcovers. The bed and bath were compact, but serviceable for a month. She got a kick out of the cast-iron tub with a clear plastic shower curtain hanging from a track on the ceiling above it. Okay, maybe *that* was the adorable part of this place. But at least there *was* Wi-Fi. Cleanliness and Wi-Fi were really her only requirements.

And it *did* have a nice view. The cottage—who was she kidding, it was a cabin—was on a narrow piece of land that jutted out into Gallant Lake. There was a cluster of these little square boxes. They were old…*really* old…summer camps that had been converted to rentals. Brittany had taken the one farthest out, so she could see water outside the windows on three sides. Clouds were low and threatening that morning, but she paid no mind to that. She'd learned storms blew up and blew over quickly here. Conrad would be expecting reports on her progress, even if it was her first week there.

She'd made contact with three of the owners on

the water side of Main Street. Four, if she counted Nate Thomas, but neither of their conversations had involved properties or selling. Stella was looking for a tenant, but she said she'd sell if the right offer came along. Bill Nichols owned the vacant diner. He'd been surprised to get a call from Brittany about buying the property, but he hadn't said no. Probably the most challenging prospect for a quick sale were the Carters with their consignment shop. Their business wasn't exactly booming, but they referred to themselves as "lifers" in Gallant Lake and said they weren't ready to retire for a while.

It was a fine line Brittany was walking, trying to keep all this under the radar of the gossip grapevine that surely existed in a small town like this. She'd told each person that she was just curious and might know someone interested in buying a business property here. Then she begged them to keep it "just between them" for now, as she was only here to visit and didn't want to be hounded by people looking to sell. That was just enough to plant the seed with each property owner that there might be competition out there—other sellers with more enticing properties, or maybe lower prices. So they'd agreed to keep things on the down low. There was no way to enforce it, of course. There was still a chance someone would tell a friend, and the friend would tell another friend, and so on. But she hoped to keep her dealings quiet until she had two or three of the properties they wanted under contract.

Later that day she made herself dinner and sat down to relax. She'd opened most of the windows and the front door to let a nice lake breeze blow through the cabin. Knowing she hadn't planned to see any clients today, she was a bit more casual, but still too citified for this place. Her pink seersucker capris and matching knit top were comfortable, but stylish. Then again, the town had a lovely clothing boutique, so she couldn't say the place had no style at all.

She took a sip of her wine, grateful the town also had a good liquor store. Her deep fuchsia toenail polish was making a statement in her sparkly flip-flops. The ones Nate Thomas had given her. She'd never been much of a flip-flop girl, even when she spent time on the Gulf Coast beaches around Tampa. But the fluorescent orange footwear made her smile for some reason. The same way that kitschy drink did the other night at the resort.

She heard a soft scuffling sound outside the screen door. It was still daylight, if fading a bit, so she didn't think it could be a wild animal poking around…or could it? What she knew about living in the mountains would fit on the back of a matchbook. Were there bears here? Badgers? Raccoons? Or worse… rats? She wasn't feeling relaxed anymore. There was the sound again. This cabin was ancient—was there a way for critters to get inside? Could it come through the screen door? That thought was enough to get her on her feet.

She'd be damned if she was going to feel intimidated by a *noise*. She was Brittany "Barracuda" Doyle, and she didn't back down from any fight. She'd learned to never blink in business, and she figured the same rules applied with wild animals. Whatever was snooping around out there was going to regret it. She picked up the kitchen broom and moved slowly to the door. She'd just scare off whatever was out there, lock herself in and get back to her wine.

She grabbed the door handle, gripping the broom with her other hand, and whipped the screen door open. To her horror, something small and furry came running past her feet and into the cabin the instant there was enough space. Brittany let out a shriek and spun around, then let out a shaky breath.

It was a smallish dog. At least…she was pretty sure it was a dog. It was possibly white under all the dirt, its long hair matted in some places and standing on end in others. It had ears that stood straight up, with tufts of hair making them look even bigger. That hair—this dog had no shortage of it—fell across one eye, à la a young Brad Pitt. She leaned over and checked. A boy. A wild-haired boy dog. Sitting in the center of her living area.

"Oh, no, you don't." She set down the broom and pointed to the door, which she was holding open.

"You need to go home. And this ain't it." He tipped his head back and forth in that adorable way dogs had… No. She could not think of this mutt as adorable. She didn't do dogs. She didn't do pets, period. She traveled too much, and they were an impractical distraction she didn't need in her life.

But this dog was unconcerned with her practicality. His feathered tail swept back and forth on the floor where he sat, and his mouth dropped open to reveal a bright pink tongue and a goofy grin. She steeled herself against his obvious charm.

"You need to go. Get out. I'm serious!" She held the door farther open. "Get out right now."

"Is everything okay here?" The male voice coming from outside made her shriek again, letting the screen door slam shut. Halfway through her scream, she realized she recognized the voice. Nate Thomas. The man was everywhere. She glared at him through the screen. He'd ditched his jeans and plaid for khaki cargo shorts and a well-worn T-shirt. He wasn't smiling. In fact, he seemed to be bristling and tense.

She'd always been of the opinion that cargo shorts were the hallmark of suburban dads trying to look hip and failing badly. Seriously, what did any man need that many loops and pockets for? Dweeb city. But for some reason, the shorts worked for Nate. Maybe because they were as well-worn and soft-looking as his T-shirt. Maybe because they hung a little low on his hips, revealing the slightest hint of an underwear waistband...red with a wide blue stripe in the elastic. A surprising bit of color for Mr. Plaid. What on earth was he doing outside her temporary home?

"You know, Nate, it's one thing to run into you at a public place like the resort. Understandable coincidence there. But I really need to know what you're doing at my front door." Her eyes narrowed. "Uninvited."

He held up his hands in innocence. "Sorry for seeming like a creeper dude. I live down at the end of Lakeshore Drive, which is just down that way." He nodded his head to the side. "Nora told me you'd rented one of Vince's places, and I was going to welcome you to the neighborhood." His expression grew more serious. "Then I heard you trying to throw someone out and got concerned. Is everything okay?"

She grinned in spite of herself.

"This place is attracting a parade of uninvited male guests tonight." She held open the screen door so he could see the dog. As soon as the dog saw Nate, he started barking, coming to stand at Brittany's side like a protector. It was cute. No, not cute. She did *not* need a dog.

Nate grinned and stepped forward to scratch the pup's chin. "I've seen this dog skulking around people's trash cans for a few weeks now. You brought him inside, huh?"

"He brought himself in. I heard a noise and opened the door, and he bolted inside. And won't leave." She put her hand on her hip and stared down at the dog, who was definitely grinning up at her. "I don't do dogs."

"It looks like maybe you do." He patted Joey's head—oh, God, she'd named the dog—and stood to face her. "He's a mess. Want some help cleaning him up? Do you have dog dishes and food? I sell pet supplies at the…"

"He is *not* a pet! At least, he's not *my* pet. I don't want a dog, no matter how cute he is…" She closed her eyes in frustration. She had to stop noticing his cuteness. "He can't stay. This is a rental, and they probably don't want pets…"

"Vince has four dogs of his own," Nate said. "Pretty sure he's not anti-dog."

"He must have owners somewhere."

"I'll ask around, but he doesn't look like anyone's beloved pet." Nate pointed out the obvious. "He hasn't been cared for. No collar. No tags. And like I said, I've seen him digging into trash around here for a few weeks now. It's not uncommon for people to dump unwanted dogs in remote neighborhoods like this."

This couldn't be happening. "If he's a stray, he won't want to be confined. He'll want to live outside, running free."

"Um…" Nate nodded toward the sofa behind her. Where Joey was curling up on a pillow, plopping his chin on his front paws, watching them adoringly. His tail waved back and forth when they looked at him. He looked very much at home. *Damn*.

"Fine." Brittany waved her hands. "I give up. Joey can stay, but only as long as I'm here. I am *not* taking this dog home to Tampa."

Nate chuckled. "Joey?"

"Yeah…that mop of hair reminds me of Brad Pitt from his *Meet Joe Black* days. So…Joey."

"Okay. Well, Joey still needs a bath. And food."

"I can handle that on my own, thanks."

"You're a real independent type, huh?"

She lifted her chin. She bore a lot of weight on these shoulders of hers, but that was okay. She was used to it. She gave him a thin smile meant to send him on his way.

"You have no idea."

He studied her face. She did her best to hold on to her I-rule-the-world expression, but there was something about this guy's dark gaze that unnerved her every time. One corner of his mouth twitched upward. She'd somehow managed to amuse him again.

"That's cute, but you're in a small town now, and we don't let people handle stuff alone. I'll be back in a bit."

And he was gone. Didn't say where to. Didn't say why he thought he had to return. Just gave her that small-town spiel and split. She heard a loud sigh behind her. Joey had stretched out across the sofa pillow and was falling asleep, his head hanging off one edge of the pillow.

Her sister would die laughing when Brittany told her that, in the span of half an hour on her first week here, she'd gained a helpful neighbor she didn't want and a mangy dog she didn't need. Things were not going according to plan, and Brittany liked it best when the plan was followed. But damn, that little dog was cute.

And frankly, so was the neighbor.

Nate told himself he was just being…helpful. That was what Gallant Lake folks did—they helped each other. Even if that meant driving into town, opening their shop, loading their van with pet supplies and driving back to a woman's house to help her adopt a dog she claimed she didn't want. It was almost dark when he got back to the cabin she'd rented from Vince.

The thought made him chuckle as he parked the van. He knew Vince had been renting out the old fishing camps, listing them on some vacation website. He'd seen a few people in and out that summer. Mostly fishermen, mountain bikers or rock climbers, looking for a cheap spot to stay with room to store their equipment. Definitely a lot less upscale than the resort, which was interesting. Brittany Doyle definitely seemed like an upscale kind of woman.

He knocked on the screen door, then hooked his

finger on the latch and opened it. His arms were full of dog dishes, dog food, dog toys and a dog bed. And shampoo, of course. Brittany called out from the bathroom, her voice sharp.

"Hello? Who's there?"

"It's Nate. I told you I'd be back. I brought goodies."

There was a pause, and he heard the laughter in her voice. "Just what every woman wants—a man bearing goodies."

"I'm afraid the goodies are for the dog." He glanced at the spotless kitchen. "Do you need anything? Did you eat?"

"Damn it, Joey, stay still." He heard splashing. "I had dinner. But honestly…I could use a hand in here."

He couldn't resist needling her. "Are you sure? I thought you had this all under control."

"Save your gloating for later, okay?"

He set everything down on the kitchen table, dug out the shampoo and went to the bathroom door. He was not prepared for the sight of Brittany on her knees next to the tub, trying to contain a highly offended, and very wet, dog. She was wearing the same pink outfit, but it was now soaking wet and clinging to her in some very interesting places. Her hair was gathered at the top of her head in a loose, floppy knot. She looked over her shoulder and arched a brow.

"Is that another thing small-town people do—eyeball each other's asses?"

His laugh surprised them both. This city lady had attitude to spare. He wasn't a big fan of attitude normally, but there was something...*sharp*...about her that appealed to him. And she had a point. He straightened, his cheeks warming.

"No... Sorry. That was hella rude."

He handed her the shampoo and scooted around to the other side of the tub to grab the dog... Joey. Things were a lot easier with two sets of hands, and Joey was a much cleaner animal ten minutes later when Nate lifted him up and wrapped him in a towel. The dog snuggled into the towel, as if afraid this sudden change in his fortune might vanish at any moment.

Brittany sprayed the tub and wiped it down as Nate dried Joey. Other than a few places where his long hair was impossibly knotted, the dog looked much better. And he seemed to know it, too. When Nate put him down, he raced around the living room a few times, shaking himself and rubbing up against furniture as if he couldn't believe his good luck. Nate grinned.

"He almost looks like an actual dog." He pointed to the kitchen table when Brittany joined him. "I brought a few things you'll need."

Her eyes went wide. "A few? Looks like you emptied the pet section. How much do I owe you?" She pulled out two bowls, filling one with water and setting it on the floor while she waited for Nate to open the bag of food. "And don't tell me 'nothing.' This is a lot more than a pair of flip-flops."

"We can settle up tomorrow at the store. I figure I'm next on your list."

Brittany froze. That was probably an asinine move on his part, but he needed to remind himself that he still had no idea why she was *vacationing* here— he glanced around the sparsely furnished cabin— or why she was spending so much time with his business neighbors in town. She finished filling the food dish and set it down for a ravenous Joey, then straightened, regaining her cool composure.

"What list?"

"You've been to the consignment shop and the hair salon, and I saw you talking with Stella about her building." He did his best to sound friendly and casual about it, rather than accusatory, but her expression told him he'd failed.

"So not only do you show up everywhere I am, you also keep track of what I do during the day?" She stared at the pile of pet supplies on her table. "You know what? I'll pay you for what I've used, but you can take the rest back. I'm not..."

Nate held up his hand to stop her.

"I'm not taking it back. And I'm sorry for how that sounded just now. It's just that this is a small..."

"A small town?" She folded her arms on her chest.

"Yeah, I got that the first twenty times you brought it up. It's not the first small town I've ever seen, Nate. I know how they work. Everybody in everybody's business. All smiles in public, then backstabbing gossip shared over coffee." She gestured in his direction. "Pretending to care, when all you really want is information."

A minute ago they'd been laughing and bathing a dog together. Now they were in opposite corners, bristling and wary. But there was something about the way her voice almost broke when she said *pretending to care* that made him dial back his anger. He'd pushed her, but he hadn't intended to hurt her. Yet somehow he knew he had.

"I *do* care." His voice leveled. "I care about this town, and I care about the people here. And yes, I get…curious…when someone new shows up and starts visiting the businesses around me. Those are my friends. Most are older than me, and I'm protective of them. I won't apologize for that." He watched Joey settle himself in the overstuffed chair, spinning three times before collapsing in an exhausted heap of hair. He looked back to Brittany. "I'm not trying to offend you, and I'm definitely not stalking you. Or gossiping about you." He pushed his conversation with Nora to the back of his mind. That was just one time. "But I gotta say, for someone with such a low opinion of small towns, I'm wondering why you said you're thinking of moving here."

Color rose on her cheeks, and she blinked a few times. Her gaze bounced around the room before returning to him.

"I'm in Gallant Lake to take a break from the rat race." Nate hated how those words rang false in his head. She seemed to be a woman who'd relish any kind of race, as long as she had a shot at winning. But he barely knew her, so he held his peace and let her continue. "And yes, I'm looking at some business properties, but not for myself. I work in real estate, and I have a friend…a client…who might be interested in a waterfront business here." That seemed more realistic to Nate. But she still seemed to be holding back. Her smile brightened. Too much? Or was he just being a jerk tonight? "In fact, he's the only reason I even *heard* of Gallant Lake. He made it…" She hesitated, her smile faltering just a bit. "He made it sound like a place I had to visit."

"So this is a business trip?"

"Sort of. I hope to get some pleasure, too." She looked over to where Joey was snoring in the chair. "I mean, I already have a dog, right?"

"What kind of business is your friend looking to open here?" He heard himself and winced. He sounded like he was interrogating her, and he rushed to clarify. "I'm just saying I know every business and business owner in town. I might be able to help."

"Maybe. But honestly, I'm exhausted." She gestured around the tiny cabin. "This place might be humble, but it's my home for the time being. And I try not to do business in my home."

"You're right. I'll tell you what. Why don't you stop by the store tomorrow when you're free, and we can talk about it during working hours. I'm serious about wanting to help." He also was very curious about what kind of business an outsider might bring to his town. "And we can settle up on the dog stuff. I'm the one who talked you into keeping him, so I'll give you a discount. Sound good?"

She nodded, but her gaze skittered around the room again. Was that a tell that she was hiding something? Or was she just a tired neighbor he should leave alone? She picked up the bright orange stuffed dog toy he'd brought over and grinned.

"It matches my flip-flops." She'd moved them to safer conversation territory, and that was fine by him. "I really do appreciate you bringing all of this. I've never had a pet and wouldn't know where to start."

"Never? Not even as a kid?"

Just like that, her smile was gone, and shutters closed behind her eyes.

"Ugh…no. We had our hands full feeding ourselves. Didn't need an extra hungry belly." She stared off into the corner, and he was pretty sure she wasn't actually seeing anything. Except maybe a glimpse into a childhood that clearly hadn't been happy.

Miss I'm-in-Control had a story behind that hard-charging attitude of hers. Nate was surprised to re-alize he was now more curious about knowing that story than knowing why she was in Gallant Lake.

Chapter Five

Brittany hadn't paid much attention to the parrot in Nate's Hardware the first time she'd come in. The damn thing scared the bejesus out of her that day, almost setting her on her ass. But she'd been quickly distracted by Nate himself. His amusement at her predicament, and his efficiency at fixing it for her. She stopped by the cage.

Nate had seemed such a gentle, easygoing guy that first day. An easy target for Conrad's plan. But there was more to Nate than his Mr. Nice Guy persona suggested. He was suspicious of her, and apparently had been right from the start. And she hadn't picked up on it. It wasn't like her to miss something like that. She was generally able to spot the skeptics right off—the ones who would righteously object to progress coming to their communities. Of course, that usually didn't happen until she was well into the process of buying properties. Nate had started watching her right away. Like his parrot.

The bird was studying her from the back corner of the cage now, softly whistling to himself before hopping closer. The cage itself was up on wooden legs and had to be four foot square and maybe five feet tall. There were multiple perches crisscrossing the cage at different angles and intervals, and toys and dishes clipped to the black metal bars. The parrot suspended himself horizontally on the side of the cage, turning his head back and forth. He whistled once before making an announcement that made her laugh out loud.

"Sale! Sale! Sale! Everything's on sale!"

Nate came out of the back office, hands on his hips.

"Hank, you're going in the stew pot if you don't quit that."

Hank ruffled his feathers. "Help! Help! Help!"

She grinned, reaching toward the cage to rub his shimmering turquoise feathers. Nate grabbed her hand, shaking his head and pointing at the sign on the cage.

My name is Hank.
My hobbies are biting and cursing.

Don't encourage me.
I'm a bad, bad bird.

"You keep a biting, cursing bird in your place of business?" She tried to ignore the little buzz of energy she felt in her hand, which Nate was still holding.

"Are you kidding? He's the main attraction. He has a very loyal following in town." Nate looked at his hand on hers and seemed surprised. He released her and nodded toward the parrot. "He doesn't really bite that often, but when he does…well, let's just say he can eat a raw carrot with that beak. And fingers poking through the bars look like carrots. He's a very hungry bird."

"Hungry bird! Hungry bird! Feed me, you lazy bast…"

"Hank! No." Nick tapped the side of the cage. "Be nice for the pretty lady."

"Pretty lady! Pretty lady! Pretty bird! Pretty bird!"

"You *are* a pretty bird, Hank," Brittany said. "And a smart one, too."

Nate rolled his eyes. He took a dried banana chip out of a paper bag near the cage and gave it to Hank through the bars. "He's too smart. My dad thought it was hysterical to teach him how to swear. A lot. I have to keep teaching him new stuff to keep him from cussing out customers."

Nate was in his usual uniform today. A plaid shirt with the sleeves rolled up, tucked into his usual jeans, with sturdy leather hiking boots. Practical. She'd come to realize it suited him. His chestnut hair was mussed, as if he'd been running his fingers through it.

"Did you break any more heels on your way here?" He was teasing. Amused by her as usual.

She shook her head. "I don't make a habit of that, so if you're thinking of relying on cobbling as a second career, you'll be disappointed." She stuck one leg out and turned it to show him her more practical footwear—sturdy, low-heeled leather pumps.

"Speaking of careers…" He was still smiling, but there was caution in his eyes.

"Yes, I know. I'm here for business today. But first, we need to settle up…" Her eyes widened. "Hey, you haven't even asked me about Joey. For all you know, I kicked him out into the dark after you left last night."

Nate smirked. "It's far more likely he spent the night on the sofa. Or perhaps in bed with you?"

She didn't answer. She didn't have to. She'd woken that morning to find Joey sprawled out on the other side of the bed, taking up an amazing amount of space and snoring. Loudly.

"Here's your tab, Brittany." He handed her a handwritten sales slip. "No hurry. It's not like I don't know where you live at the moment." He leaned against Hank's cage. "And now for *your* business. Tell me about this friend-slash-client of yours."

This was the part of her job she hated. Or hated the *most*. Her brows gathered. Lately, it had been hard to think of what she *liked* about it, other than the really big paychecks. Which paid for Ellie's insulin *and* tuition. Those paychecks were Brittany's security. And if the job pushed her into some…murky… moral territory, that was just the price she had to pay. Including telling half-truths to a guy she was starting to like.

"I do a lot of high-end real-estate deals," she said. "And when you deal with rich folks, things get weird." She shrugged. She'd learned long ago to keep the lie as close to the truth as possible. It made it less complicated. "The rich really *are* different. And demanding. And secretive." *No lies there.* "Sometimes they don't want me to know *why* they want what they want. This is one of those times." Okay, that was a lie. She glanced away, watching Hank chew on a hunk of white stuff mounted to the cage bars. It seemed to be made for that purpose, since it was covered with deep grooves from his beak. "This is one of those clients. He sent me to Gallant Lake and told me to quietly find a small business on the water." Or *all* of the small businesses on the water.

Nate stared at her in silence. She'd negotiated with a lot of tough customers over the years, but he had a way of making her feel like squirming. Without saying a word. She took a deep, steadying breath.

"So yes, I am talking to your neighbors on Main Street. And now I'm talking to you…"

He straightened with a soft laugh. "Save your breath, Brittany. This place is *not* for sale. My great-great-grandfather started selling nails and screws in this spot in the 1800s. There's not an offer in the world that would get me to sell."

She looked around the empty store. "Because it's making you so much money?"

"There's more to life than money. Your rich clients may not know that, but I do." More to life than money? It was a noble statement, but she knew the truth. Without money, there *was* no life. She'd learned that at a very early age.

She put her hand on her hip, reminding herself she needed to win this guy over and convince him to sell. How could she find the right button to push?

"So this store…this very quiet store…is your passion?"

A flicker of doubt crossed his face. A-*ha*. She'd found his soft spot on the first try.

"That's a no. What *is* your passion?"

He crossed his arms. "That was *not* a no. My passion, as you call it, is preserving history. I preserve it here at the store that's been in my family for five generations, and I preserve it in this town. In fact, I'm president of the Gallant Lake Preservation Society. We took the Gallant Lake Resort to court when Blake Randall threatened to make it into a casino. In fact, we took *him* to court when he wanted to raze a historic home next to the resort. And we won." His voice had grown harder as he spoke. "So you might want to let your client know that."

Damn. She'd run into community organizers before, but she hadn't anticipated that Nate might be the enemy. She kept her calm, friendly smile in place.

"Impressive. The town is lucky to have you, Nate. But community service can't be your only passion. What do you love doing?" She stepped closer. "And I mean *doing*, not the esoteric 'fighting for' stuff."

The bell at the door chimed as a couple walked in. Hank ruffled his feathers, whistled once, then greeted them.

"Hi! Hello! Hell-o-o! Hello!"

Brittany stepped back to let Nate greet his customers. They said they were there for the lights they'd bought. Nate picked up a large box near the door, and she could see what looked like the top of a large brass chandelier. She looked around the store, wondering where his lighting department was. She saw light bulbs, but that was it.

The man pulled a smaller sconce out of the box and they admired a label on the back of it. Nate had an energy to his voice that was brand-new to her.

"After our email conversation," Nate said, "I did some more digging amd found this smaller pair in the company's 1926 catalog. That tracks, because the old house I salvaged them from was built in '26." His face fell. "I wish I could have pulled more from there before they tore it down." He patted the sconce in his hand as if it were a living thing. "But knowing these babies will have a good home makes me feel better."

The couple gushed over the lights, telling Nate they were restoring a historic home in Lake George and the lights would be going in the dining room and hallway. He asked questions about their home's history, his eyes bright with interest. They were talking crown moldings and heart pine floors and original windows and then she lost interest in the words. She was just watching Nate.

He was animated. Energized. She'd thought he was so laid-back, but seeing him now... He seemed lit up from the inside. His hands were gesturing; his smile was bright. He thanked them for following his website, and the couple asked him to be on the lookout for a mantel clock. Brittany smiled. She'd found his passion. Nate had a second business selling antiques. And he liked doing it. Maybe she could convince him to do it full-time and let the hardware store go.

After the Cuppermans left, Nate looked for Brittany. She wasn't by Hank's cage. Then he spotted her in the back, staring up at the porcelain signs hanging on the back wall with prices attached. There were some "smalls" back there, too—vintage metal toys, old bottles and some decorative odds and ends. She was examining a small porcelain piece, hand-painted with tiny roses and decorated with enamel.

"It's a hat-pin holder," he said.

She frowned, examining the small holes in the top of the six-inch piece.

"Hat pin? Oh, like back in the Victorian days?"

He reached past her to a small box on the shelf and pulled out a long metal pin with a blue bead of glass on top of it. He put it in one of the holes in the porcelain holder.

"This piece is probably early 1900s. Women still wore hats a lot, especially to church and special occasions. Their hat-pin holder would sit on their dressing table so they could select whatever pin matched their outfit."

She smiled as she set the pin holder back on the shelf, with the hat pin still in it. "You sell antiques along with your hardware. Where do you find them? Other dealers?"

His eyes scanned the shelves. He needed to do some dusting out here.

"Only if I need something specific. I prefer to go picking."

"What's *picking*?"

"That's where the fun is. I go to barn sales and estate sales, or sometimes just walk up to someone's place and ask to poke around their outbuildings. Just

like that show on the History Channel." She gave
him a blank look. Yeah, she probably wasn't the type
to curl up and watch a couple of Iowa guys climb
around haylofts on television. "Never mind. You'll
just have to trust me that it's fun. You have to dig
through a lot of dirt and junk, but when you find a
treasure, it makes it all worth it." He thought for a
moment. "You asked earlier what my passion was,
and I guess it's picking."

He picked up a metal windup toy car, complete
with rubber tires and a little guy at the wheel, gog-
gles on and looking like he was ready to race. "I
found this one shoved to the back of a shelf in an old
barn, behind a bunch of oil cans and auto parts. The
doors open…" He tugged on the tiny door to show
her. "See? The driver comes out, and most of the time
he's missing when you find the car. But this one's
intact—original paint, all the little pieces. It was
like finding a gold nugget in an abandoned mine."

Brittany was giving him a funny look. She was in
her all-business attire today. Linen trousers, a crisp
cotton shirt and a tailored beige jacket. Her hair was
pulled back in a ponytail, tied with her one nod to
whimsy—a bright yellow silk scarf with bold pink-
and-white flowers. Nate couldn't help thinking he
missed the soaking-wet pink capris from last night.
Her mouth slid into a slanted grin.

"This little toy felt like a nugget of gold to you?
Have you ever *seen* a gold nugget?" She took the car

from him, staring at it dubiously. "Because this is not anything like that. It's a child's toy."

"It's a piece of history," he answered, taking the car from her and setting it carefully on the shelf. "It's something you can't get anymore. There's a limited number still left in the world, which makes each one unique. I look at picking antiques as rescuing things like this from today's disposable society. If no one does that, we lose a part of our past."

Brittany's eyes were wide. "So you're some kind of superhero for old stuff?"

He chuckled. "Something like that, yeah. Luckily, there are still people out there who collect these things. When I sell something, I know it's going to a good home where it will be valued, not shoved in a corner."

She blinked a few times, her face going pale. Her lips parted as if he'd just knocked the wind out of her. What had he said? He was just talking about selling antiques, and good homes, where things were valued… *Oh, damn.* She'd said something last night about her family not being able to feed themselves easily, much less a pet. Maybe things were even more dire than a lack of food, if she connected with him saying something was valued in a home.

"Hey…" He put his hand on her shoulder, waiting for her to look up at him. "The lesson here is that everything, and everyone, deserves to have a home where they're appreciated for what they are.

And it's never too late." He nodded toward the toy car. "That car was covered with dirt and cobwebs, and look at it now."

Her eyes were shinier than usual, and she gave him a hard smile that hardly trembled at all. "I don't know why you think I need the greeting-card sentiments, Nate. I brushed off my cobwebs a long time ago." She gestured down, a touch of bitterness creeping into her voice. "And look at me now, right?"

He *was* looking at her. What he saw surprised him. He'd had a hint that she had a story behind the corporate veneer, but now he saw her as a double image, with the uptight, put-together real-estate broker layered over the pink-clad woman in bright orange flip-flops and her hair piled on her head, washing a dog in a claw-foot tub. There was a disconnect between the images, and he wondered if she felt it. Or had she fooled herself into believing her own marketing spiel?

Before he could respond, the door chimed. It was Darius, reporting for work. Nate had watched the seventeen-year-old grow up in Gallant Lake. His mom, Maya Malone, had him when she was in high school and refused her parents' insistence that she give him up. She'd fought hard to raise a good kid while little more than a kid herself, and she'd succeeded. She was married to the mayor now, and the two women had adopted a set of twin girls a few years back. Darius adored his new baby sisters, but he was also thankful for any opportunity to get out of a house filled with women. Nate had a feeling that was why he'd asked for a job at the hardware store. Lots of testosterone in this old place.

He introduced Brittany and Darius, with Hank whistling and laughing in the background. Hank loved Darius, mainly because the kid was always teaching him new stuff to say. Some of it Nate approved of. Some…not so much. But he was a good worker and customers liked him. His presence gave Nate a chance to get out of the building once in a while to go picking or just run errands. He watched Darius showing Brittany the computer inventory system the teenager had installed and maintained. Nate appreciated the benefits of technology, but he was a traditional guy through and through. He preferred records he could touch.

As the noon hour rolled around, more customers wandered in. Some were tourists from the resort, looking to take selfies in the quaint old hardware store. Some were regulars, looking for actual hardware items—hinges, nails, paintbrushes. And through it all, Brittany stayed. When it got busy, she sat in the corner, on the old Stickley armchair he'd found hanging from a hook in someone's barn. Nate had refinished it and put a new leather seat on it. Brittany sat on it like it was a throne, watching everything going on in the store.

He had a strong hunch this was more than casual

curiosity. From the focus in her eyes, she could have been some business consultant doing a study on him. Did she really think he was fooled into thinking she'd given up on the idea of him selling the store? He may not know her well, but he knew she wasn't the type to give up that quickly. That didn't bother him. It wasn't like he was going to change his mind. But one thing *did* bother him: this mystery client of hers. What kind of business would someone be that eager to bring to little Gallant Lake? Some franchised fast-food place? She said the client wanted waterfront. This entire side of Main Street was waterfront. But how much waterfront did they want? Why was she talking to *everyone*? If all she needed was one property, there were several on the market.

He opened the door to Hank's cage and let the bird hop onto his shoulder while he poured food into his dish. Hank was in a whistling mood today, making music almost nonstop.

"Can I hold him?" Brittany was at his side. Her defenses were relaxed again, her focus on the noisy bird and not business. Nate liked her this way, but he still didn't trust her. Something didn't add up. But the sparkle in her eyes right now made him push his suspicions aside.

He smiled. "Sure. Hold your arm straight out and get ready. He's heavier than you think."

She did as he said, and Hank gladly jumped over to her, quickly moving up to her shoulder to pick at the bright bow in her hair. Nate went to get the bird, but Brittany pulled back.

"He's fine. It's an old scarf anyway. Hey!" Hank had tugged some of her hair along with the scarf. "Is he…is he *laughing*?"

Nate nodded. "Technically, he's not laughing, but it's one of his favorite sounds. He does that when he's happy."

"So he likes me?" Brittany's expression faltered so briefly Nate wasn't sure he'd seen it. But he thought he saw a flash of vulnerability there. She wanted to be liked.

"Yeah, he likes you. And your bright scarf." Nate hesitated, but couldn't hold back the words he wanted to squelch. "I like you, too."

She looked up in surprise, her eyes softening. "You sure it's not just the bright scarf?"

He chuckled. "I'm sure. But I'm still never selling this store."

Something clicked into place in her eyes. It looked a lot like a silent *challenge accepted*.

"Never say never, Nate. Things change. People change. Minds change."

Hank laughed on her shoulder. "Ha ha ha ha ha!"

Nate nodded, reaching out his hand to put the bird back in his cage.

"I agree, Hank. Your friend Brittany is being very silly right now. She doesn't know how much I hate change, does she?"

Chapter Six

"Brittany, you said one sugar and extra cream, right?"

Nora Peyton was behind the counter at Gallant Brew, pouring coffee. The coffee shop was quiet, in the lull between breakfast people and lunch customers. Brittany had started stopping by over the past week during that quiet hour to chat with Nora. Some days, like today, Nora's cousins and friends gathered at the same time.

"Yes, thanks," she answered, taking a seat at the table. Nora's two cousins were already there. Amanda Randall, petite and cheery, was the wife of the owner of the Gallant Lake Resort. Mel Brannigan owned the town's one and only boutique, Five and Design.

A baby carrier sat on the chair next to her, where her newborn son Patrick was sound asleep.

Nora brought a tray of coffees to the table. She was just sitting when the front door opened. Brittany recognized the tall blonde, Mackenzie Wallace, from the liquor store up the street, but she didn't know the brunette with her. Nora introduced them—the quiet woman was Cassie Zetticci. She worked at the resort, and Nora explained she used to live in the apartment above the coffee shop. An engagement ring sparkled on her finger. She saw Brittany looking at it and confirmed she was engaged to the chief of security for Randall Resorts International, Nick West.

Once everyone had their beverage of choice and had pulled tables together to make room for all to sit, Mel lifted her cup in a mock toast.

"Welcome to Gallant Lake, Brittany! I heard you're in real estate. The more strong professional women in this town, the better."

"Well…I'm just visiting…"

Nora gave her a curious look over the rim of her cappuccino. "I thought you said you were thinking of relocating? That's why you rented a place here for so long, right?"

This wasn't the first time Brittany had let her guard slip since arriving here. It was as if the mountain air was interfering with her ability to maintain her professional focus. She recovered with a wide smile.

"Well, yes, but it's only a possibility, not a sure

thing. I don't know if I'm ready to give up my Florida beaches."

Mel sighed. "I hear that. I lived in Miami for a while, and when winter comes blowing in around here, I dream of those beautiful beaches."

"But you're also here on business, right?" Mack Wallace reached for a cookie from the tray Nora's employee, Cathy, had just delivered to the table. "I'm engaged to the police chief, and Dan heard you were talking to a few business owners."

She concentrated on keeping her smile in place. The small-town grapevine was catching up with her plans sooner than anticipated. But it was bound to happen at some point, so she'd have to shift her story a little.

"I have a client who might be interested in opening a business here. He wants waterfront property. So I'm combining my personal and business lives while I'm here." She leaned forward, and several of the women leaned in, too. "But I'm not even sure the guy will pull the trigger. And before you ask, he won't tell me what the business is. Dealing with these eccentric types is enough to drive me to drink, I swear." She looked out the window, across Main Street to the small gazebo near the lake, and off to the left, Nate's store. "Don't shoot me for saying this, but it seems more business—more people—would be a good thing, right? For your own businesses?"

Mel and Mack looked at each other and nodded.

"It's true," Mack said. "More traffic would help the bottom line, but we don't want to lose what makes Gallant Lake special. I mean, I'm the only one here who actually grew up in this place. I'd hate to see it turn into some honky-tonky tourist town."

Nora agreed. "Or some generic, gentrified suburb. It's a fine line between having the right amount of businesses and losing the town's personality completely."

Brittany looked around the table. "So all of you other than Mack came here from somewhere else? How did *that* happen?" She'd only come here because Conrad told her to. She couldn't imagine what the draw was for these professional women.

Amanda smiled, nudging Nora's shoulder. "I started it, right? I came here for an interior design job and ended up marrying the boss. Then Nora's daughter came to visit me and fell for a boy who lived here. When they ended up pregnant, Nora bought the coffee shop to be closer to them. And ended up marrying her neighbor, the boy's father, Asher. Mel came here because *we* were here."

"That's true," Mel said. "But I stayed because Gallant Lake felt…safe…for me." She glanced at Brittany. "I was newly sober and struggling. This place just felt like home for me. So much so that I chose it over following the love of my life to LA." She looked down at the sleeping baby near her side. "Luckily, he came to his senses and came back to join me here."

"This does feel like a safe place," Cassie said. She'd been quiet so far, and Brittany hadn't been able to figure out if she was shy or standoffish. But her sweet smile said it was the former. "Cathy is my aunt." She nodded toward the coffee counter, where Cathy was stacking cups and counting sugar packets. "I needed to…hide. From my ex." She raised her chin, summoning up an inner strength Brittany couldn't help but admire. "I came here and got a job at the resort and had a little workplace romance along the way. Nick was my real safe place, but the town—" she looked at the women sitting with her "—and the friends I made here gave me strength, too."

After a beat of silence, Nora reached over and patted Brittany's hand. "So be careful, girl, or you'll get caught up in the magic of Gallant Lake and end up living here forever."

"I don't really do *forever*. I like to stay on the move."

A puffy white cloud slid across the sky, releasing the sun's warmth it had been hiding. The buildings she'd first thought of as sad when she'd arrived now looked…friendly in the morning light. The faded clapboard buildings were soft and simple. The brick ones, like the hardware store and Nora's coffee shop, seemed strong and understated. If she *was* going to settle down in some cozy little town, this one had its appeal. But this life wasn't for her.

"She sounds like you, Mel! Big world traveler

resisting the pull of our little mountain hamlet."
Amanda finished her coffee and glanced at her
watch. "My daughter Maddy has a doctor appoint-
ment in an hour. She got into some poison ivy and
she's just miserable. I'm hoping we can get her some
prescription lotion or something, poor kid."

She said her goodbyes and the women talked
about their families and husbands or fiancés. Something Brittany didn't see on her agenda for a very
long time. She tried to ignore that little voice telling
her she didn't have that much time left. She was only
thirty-four. There was plenty of time. Wasn't there?

"And speaking of hot guys, Brittany, I saw you at
Nate's store the other day." Nora gave a broad wink.
"Was that business or pleasure?"

Mack nodded, a wicked glimmer in her eye. "Oh,
yeah—Dan told me he saw you two walking a dog
together the other night near Dan's place?"

A buzz of oohs and aahs went around the table.
Mel's eyes went wide. "You were at his *place*? That's
not far from our house. Are you guys a thing?"

"No!" Brittany practically shouted the word,
which just amused the other women. "Seriously, so
not a thing. That was a fluke."

She actually wasn't so sure. It was quite a coincidence when Nate appeared on Lakeshore Drive just
as Brittany was walking Joey a few days ago. With
no gym in town, the dog gave her a reason to get out
and get moving. He was surprisingly good on a leash,

happily trotting at her side as she kept up a brisk pace. And just like that, Nate was striding toward her from the opposite direction. He'd joined them for a while, explaining his house was at the end of the road. He pointed it out—a simple square house, well kept and nicely landscaped. It was painted dark red, with tan trim and black shutters. Traditional, just like Nate.

They'd parted at his driveway after an awkward silence. She half wanted him to invite her in, and he seemed to half want to invite her in, but it didn't happen. She liked the guy, and he said he liked her, too. But that didn't mean he trusted her. He couldn't seem to be in her presence more than ten minutes without asking about her client and quizzing her on what properties she'd seen. She had the story down pat, but she could tell he didn't quite buy it. And yet he never accused her of anything. He just gave her that disappointed look and kept digging for the truth.

"Oh, wow," Mack laughed. "Look at those dreamy eyes. Our nerdy Nate has an admirer!"

She sat straight. "He's not nerdy."

The women all looked at each other, eyebrows raised in unison. Nora tipped her head to the side. "Have you seen him in those black-rimmed glasses?"

Yes, she definitely had. She'd stepped into the store to get more dog treats and caught him at his computer, listing some antique hood ornament on his website. With the plaid shirt, the glasses and his brown hair practically standing on end, he hadn't looked like a nerd to her. He'd looked like sex on a stick. The rush of desire she'd felt came out of nowhere. All she could think of was him taking those glasses off nice and slow. And then the shirt. And then *her* shirt…

She gave herself a quick mental shake. She'd been without a man for too long. That was why she was having these silly cravings for *this* man. Up until now, she'd been perfectly happy concentrating on her career so she could pay her sister's bills. But there was something about Nate's steady, gentle calm that made her think of other things. And that was dangerous.

Nate told himself it wasn't like he was driving out of his way to go by Brittany's place almost every night. It was on his way home. Sort of. He had to drive right past Long Point, like he was doing now. And it was no big deal to turn down Long Point Road. Which was a short dead end… He rolled his eyes at himself. There was no other reason for him to go down a dead-end road she happened to live on.

Except…Vince was out of town, working the state fair in Syracuse. And Vince was a friend…an acquaintance, at least. So it made sense that Nate would drive by and check Vince's camps once in a while. Every day. For a week. He slowed at the curve before the camps.

Not that he stopped and walked around or anything. He wasn't stalking the woman. It was just that he'd heard her cabin was the only one rented this month, which meant she was alone out there. There were a few other houses on the road, but they were set back, and if Brittany needed anything… He pulled his van to the side of the road and stopped.

He was screwed. He was sure this woman was up to something more than just casually looking at businesses in town "for a friend." But he'd seen ripples of something else in her. Behind her stories was…a real story. Behind her brittleness was something… softer? No, that wasn't right. She was tough. She was also vulnerable. And she seemed to hate that.

Nate slapped the steering wheel in frustration. Now he was trying to be some sort of psychoanalyst. For a complete stranger. He was losing it. He'd been watching her flit around town for two weeks now, in and out of businesses, taking pictures, laughing with Nora and the ladies at the coffee shop, even stopping by his store once in a while. Mainly to talk to Hank and poke at Nate about how he loved antiques more than hardware. He knew what she was doing. She was trying to get him to think about selling the place. As if. He should be furious about it. Instead, he admired the game she was playing. And she seemed to know it. She wasn't putting a hard sell on him, as if she knew he was a lost cause. But still…she kept stopping by.

And not just the store. She'd walked that wild-haired little dog Joey past his house a couple of times, even *after* she found out it was his place. He'd joined her the one time, but felt weird about doing it again. It wasn't like they were a thing. They weren't even friends, quite. She was a visitor to his town, and she was up to something. And he couldn't get her off his mind.

"Are you lost?" He heard her voice asking the question. Yeah, he was lost.

"Nate. Are you okay?" He blinked and turned to the open passenger window. Where Brittany stood, looking at him like she thought he was crazy. He was parked in a van on her street, with a direct line of sight to her cabin. He was lucky she wasn't calling the cops.

"Uh…yeah. Sorry. I…thought I forgot to…feed Hank before I left, so I was going to…you know… turn around…but now I realize I *did* feed him, and…"

She leaned on the door, amusement dancing in her eyes. "And did you realize that before or after you turned down the dead-end road I live on? Were you coming to tell me you're having second thoughts about putting a price on your store?"

He laughed. "Dream on. Okay, you caught me. I was coming over to…" His mind spun, trying to come up with something plausible. "To invite you to go picking with me tomorrow!"

That was not at all what he'd intended to say.

Her jaw dropped. "To invite me *where*?"

He was in it now.

"You're always asking me about the antiques and where they come from and all that, so I thought I'd show you. There's a barn sale out by the llama farm, and Mrs. Kennedy said I could look through her grandfather's place again if I wanted." It was one of his favorite spots—the old house had been closed up for decades, just the way it was when old man Kennedy died. His grandchildren had fought about the property for ages, but Blanche Kennedy had managed to get them to agree to let her handle selling everything off. "It's like walking into a time capsule. You'll love it."

She disappeared out of sight for a moment, then straightened with the dog in her arms.

"First, I will probably *not* love it. And second… there's a *llama* farm?"

There was a childish quality to the way she'd asked that last question that made him forget he'd just been winging it with that invitation. Now all he wanted to do was spend the next day showing Brittany the *real* Gallant Lake. He winked at her and put the van in Reverse.

"I'll pick you up at nine. We're gonna get dirty, so…" He saw the laughter in her eyes and shook his head. "You know what I mean. Don't wear all that fancy stuff. Be practical."

She stepped back and turned away, tossing her last words over her shoulder.

"I've got just the thing. But you better show me llamas, mister."

Chapter Seven

Brittany looked at her reflection and smiled. She knew she had to have the plaid cotton shirt at Mel's boutique the minute she saw it. It reminded her of Nate. Would he get it when he saw her? Or was he oblivious to the fact that he wore plaid so much? She was even wearing jeans. Not mom jeans, of course, but stretchy jeans with artfully worn spots and holes. It was funny in a way. She'd grown up wearing thrift-store bargains that came with holes no designer had placed. She'd hated it. Now she was paying two hundred dollars for ones that had holes *on purpose*.

She fed Joey and made sure he had water. The mutt had settled into being a house dog quickly, happy as a clam staying home while Brittany was out, as long as he had food and access to the sofa for naps. He was living a good life these days. She'd miss him when she went home to Tampa. Which would be soon, if things kept going her way.

The Thompsons were thinking about selling. Stella Cortland was all in, eager to get her business sold. Louise DiAngelo was on board, too, although Louise was a bit like Nate—skeptical and questioning. Brittany was doing her best to get everyone to stay quiet about the potential offers, but she didn't know how much longer that would last. She had a call scheduled with Conrad that week. But first…a day spent with Nate. And llamas.

He laughed as soon as he saw her. "Nice shirt. Good thing I broke pattern, or we'd look like picker twins."

He was wearing a faded T-shirt instead of plaid today. The same shirt he'd worn the night he and Joey had shown up at her door. The soft one that looked so good on him.

They started at the barn sale. Nate said they needed to be there early because it was open to the public and things would go fast. They drove up and out of Gallant Lake, through a rolling countryside dotted with old farms and newer homes. The trees were just starting to change color, with splashes of gold and red among the green.

"It's beautiful out here."

Nate nodded. "It is. I mean…it's home to me, but

I'm still amazed sometimes about how pretty it is. How lucky I am to live here."

"How much you don't want it to change?"

He gestured toward the view on the other side of the windshield. "Why would I want to see this change?"

There was a large modern house up on the side of the hill, and she pointed to it. "That house is beautiful, and it's not old."

He shook his head. "It's not just about stuff being old. It's about respecting tradition. That's my friend Wyatt's house. He built it on land that's been in his family for seventy years."

"I think you keep changing your rules. It's all very fuzzy logic to me."

He turned onto a dirt driveway that led up to a large barn where a few cars and trucks were already parked. There were tables set up outside, covered with what looked like dusty old junk to Brittany. But Nate nearly bounced out of the van, hurrying over to start digging through metal tools and signs like a kid digging through Christmas toys under the tree. She followed slowly, more fascinated by the people than by the stuff.

Customers were looking through the things on the tables and large items, like furniture and—was that an antique gas pump?—that were scattered across the lawn outside the barn doors. Assuming this…stuff… was the treasure Nate had been so enthusiastic about, there wasn't much competition between the people shopping. In fact, there was a sense of community. One woman held up an oil can and called to Nate, asking if he had that one already. He nodded and thanked her, and they both went back to searching...or picking, as Nate had called it.

Two other men, one older than the other, were examining an old white table with an enameled metal top. The older man was saying that it would have been used in a farm kitchen, where the metal top would be handy for butchering meat or sorting vegetables from the garden. The younger man nodded, said he had a perfect spot for it in his family room to hold electronics. The older guy just shrugged and agreed it could work for that, too.

She walked toward Nate, who was explaining to a young couple what some kitchen utensils had been used for, including a hand mixer operated by turning the handle to spin the beaters.

"And this, believe it or not, is an ice tray." He lifted the dangerous-looking insert, with a long metal handle and little blades that presumably formed the cubes. "You'd have to pull on this lever to pop the cubes loose and get them out. My grandmother used to make me do it because she jumped every time it popped."

The young couple picked up the box of kitchen items and thanked Nate as they went to make their purchase.

"Is the person selling all of this a friend of yours?" Brittany asked.

"Not a close friend. I know them, but not that well. Why?"

"I just wondered why you're working so hard to help other customers buy stuff. You didn't want that box?"

He nodded, reaching for a square wire basket with three old milk bottles in it. "Sure I did. I'm always on the lookout for smalls like that. Kitchen collectibles sell well and don't take a lot of shelf space."

"Then why did you answer their questions? You gave them enough information to encourage them to buy it out from under you."

His head tilted to the side and he looked puzzled by what she was saying. Then his eyes went wide and he grinned.

"Ah…you think I should have played dumb and let them walk away so I could have it for myself?"

"Basically…yeah."

"That couple told me they wanted to hang the tools on the kitchen wall in their house, which they inherited from her aunt and uncle. They've remodeled the place, but want to honor its heritage, too."

She had no idea what he was getting at.

"So?"

"So…they'll appreciate those pieces. And that's my foundational goal, to make sure history is preserved. Tradition honored. That box is going to a good home."

She threw her hands in the air. "That box could have been inventory for your business!"

"Maybe. But all that stuff probably came out of the same kitchen. And they're keeping the set together. That means something. I'm glad to see it."

They stared at each other until she shook her head.

"I don't understand your business model."

Nate picked up a small tin sign for baking soda. It was bright blue and white, with just a bit of rust around the edges. "If I can find good homes for pieces and make a little money for myself, that's fine. But this was never about that for me. I started picking with my grandfather, and picking is more about the stories we can preserve than it is about money."

She started to object, then waved him off. They were two different people when it came to business. He ended up buying an oil can with a motorcycle on it, a wooden display for thread, the baking soda sign and a small metal dump truck toy. She found a painted metal tray with a picture of a woman staring into a mirror with cosmetics on the dressing table in front of her, along with a bottle of cola. Her hair and feather-trimmed robe suggested it was from the 1930s. Brittany thought it would be a fun gift for her sister.

Nate looked at it when she was waiting to pay. He saw the twenty-dollar price tag and frowned. "Are you buying this as an investment or because you like it?"

"I like it. She reminds me of my sister. Why?"

"It's a reproduction. You see that a lot with advertising pieces, especially with soft drinks." The woman at the cash box greeted Nate warmly. He nodded, then pointed at Brittany. "You know that's not vintage, Eleanor. How about knocking a few bucks off the price?"

"Sure, hon." She took in Brittany's designer jeans and her Dooney & Bourke leather bag. "How about fifteen?"

Brittany was already pulling out the bills when Nate said, "How about ten?"

Eleanor sighed, but she didn't seem distressed. "How about twelve?"

"Deal," he answered.

As they walked back to the van, Brittany looked over to Nate.

"I'd have paid fifteen, you know. She's got to get rid of this stuff, and she deserves to make…"

"Eleanor's a picker like me, except she hits more auctions than house sales. Doesn't like getting dirty. She has a barn sale like this once a month in the good weather. And I guarantee you she didn't pay more than a couple bucks for that tray. She did just fine at ten dollars."

Brittany wasn't one to want some man to negotiate on her behalf, but she had the feeling Nate didn't do it as a control thing. He did it because he had her back. It was something new for her. And she liked it.

The llama farm was next, as promised. Brittany had never been within fifty feet of an actual llama, much less pet one and bury her fingers in their thick coat. Nate kept teasing her that one of them was going to spit at her, but luckily, they never did. The place was busy, since it was a summer weekend. But the owners knew Nate—of course—and allowed them to go into the barns and see the behind-the-scenes stuff. They saw a shy brown-and-white mama llama who got stressed by weekend crowds, so she and her adorable baby, called a cria, were moved inside on the weekends where things were quiet. She seemed very content to have Nate and Brittany petting her while her cria bounced around her like he had pogo sticks for legs.

There was a very aggressive male llama at the end of the barn. Nate explained that "Jack-o" had come to the farm with a bad attitude and had refused to shed it. But he sired beautiful babies, so the owners had created a large indoor area for Jack-o to use that kept him away from guests and other llamas. When the tour hours were over, he had a large, and very sturdy, outdoor pen to gallop around in. Nate wouldn't let Brittany near the enclosure, but he did grab some alfalfa hay and extend it through the enclosure openings for Jack-o to grab at.

They finished their tour by walking the outdoor

trails that wound through the paddocks and pastures, where dozens of llamas grazed or napped. The view was beautiful, with Gallant Lake barely visible in the distance. Nate helped Brittany up to sit on a wooden fence, first checking to be sure no llamas were in biting or spitting distance. She looked around the well-kept farm and sighed.

"This is so peaceful. It's like I can feel my heart rate slowing, just by sitting here." It was true. The perpetual tension in her shoulders and back had been getting less and less the longer she stayed in Gallant Lake. And this day, with farms and antiques and llamas and Nate… Well, it felt completely foreign and very nearly perfect.

Nate rested his chin on his hands on the top of the fence. "It's great up here. I love the water, but the farms around here just roll and weave among the hills and create a rhythm that's hard to resist."

"That's pretty poetic for a hardware guy."

He went still. "Don't do that today, Britt. Don't try to convince me I don't belong in a hardware store. That store is my life, and I promised my grandfather I'd keep it going."

She'd broken the moment, and she hated that. She put her hand down on his shoulder.

"I promise you that wasn't what I was trying to do. I know you can be kind and sometimes stubborn and a little bit stalkerish in your determination to keep an eye on me." The corner of his mouth twitched.

"But I hadn't seen your poetic side until now. It suits you. Just like the store suits you."

And in that moment, with a crisp breeze rustling the dying leaves in the nearby oak tree, she realized he really did belong in that store. And there was no way she was going to…or wanted to…convince him to sell. It didn't matter that it was her job to do so. She wasn't going to do it. Not to Nate. Which presented a whole array of problems, none of which she wanted to deal with today.

"Is that the same grandfather you used to go picking with? Tell me about him."

She'd never known her grandparents. She'd certainly never built her life around a promise to one of them. Extended families were something she learned about in movies, not in real life.

Nate looked out over the hills with a warm smile, his eyes going tender and distant, as if he was enjoying a memory.

"Grandpa was a tough old dude. Shorter than me. Not all that impressive to look at, but he was strong as an ox. He could carry a half keg of nails on each shoulder when he was in his sixties. Just like his daddy did. And his granddaddy." He glanced at her. "You want to know why the history of Gallant Lake is so important to me? It's because my ancestors basically built the place. The hardware was the second business in town, right after the saloon, which is long gone. The building is one of the originals.

Grandpa cared about that legacy, and he taught me to care, too."

"And your father?"

Nate barked out a laugh that had no humor to it.

"I'm afraid the legacy skipped a generation there. Dad couldn't have cared less. He went to college in the early '60s and became a bit of a revolutionary. Down with the establishment. Build a new world on the ashes of the old one." He lifted a shoulder. "It's not that his ideals were all bad—he wanted a better world for everybody. But he wanted it at the expense of everything his own father had worked for. As much as he claimed to hate everything about the 'old ways,' he brought my mom to Gallant Lake to raise me here, where he'd been raised. But he and Grandpa fought all the time. About the business. About politics. About the town. My father had a contrary streak in him that just got worse as he got older."

Nate rubbed the back of his neck, staring at nothing. His brows were low and tense. The memories weren't as happy now.

"It wasn't all on Dad. Grandpa was set in his ways. He wouldn't let Dad change anything in the store, and the place started to slide because the two of them couldn't agree on a single thing. The resort was facing foreclosure back then. The town was drying up. Dad started going to Atlantic City every weekend. Gambling gave him the thrill he'd never found in Gallant Lake."

He stopped, still staring into the past. Brittany waited, half regretting that she'd asked and half fascinated to see this side of Nate. To learn his story. As calm as he always seemed to be, he'd had pain in his life. She could relate to that.

He shuddered, then blinked up at her with a lukewarm smile.

"Sorry, I don't know why I just spewed all of that at you. I'm worse than a spitting llama." He reached for her hand. "We should get going. The Kennedy place doesn't have power, and we don't want to be crawling around all that junk in the dark."

She hopped down to the ground. He was done sharing, and she was okay with that, even though the story wasn't finished. She had the feeling he'd gone as far as he could go right now. Further than he'd intended to, for sure. She flashed him a smile to let him know she was on board.

"What do you mean, junk?" She nudged his arm. "I thought we were picking treasures?"

They started walking down the hill toward the parking lot. "The farm we're going to has been deserted for years. And the old guy was practically a hoarder. I'm afraid we'll have to get past some junk to find that treasure I like so much. But it's in there."

It's in there.

She'd just seen some of what he had inside, and it was more a treasure than she'd expected. Despite the sadness of his father's struggles, that past had somehow built the man Nate was now. It felt a step too far to call that treasure, but the thought insisted on rattling around her mind as she followed him to the parking lot. Unexpected treasure.

It was a quiet drive to the old Kennedy place. The only sound in the van came from the few things they'd purchased at the barn sale rattling around in the back of the van. Nate couldn't believe he'd dumped all that stuff about his father on Brittany back at the llama farm. He barely talked about it with his closest friends, much less a near stranger. Now that he'd brought it up, sour memories churned inside his chest. At the same time, he felt an odd sense of peace, too. As if he'd lifted a relief valve just long enough to let off some steam and ease the pressure of keeping all of that bottled up.

He glanced at Brittany, who didn't seem conflicted at all. Her chin rested on her hand, and her elbow was propped on the van door. She was watching the farms roll by, and she looked...content. The little buzz of energy she always carried was gone for the moment. Her hair was pulled back into a low ponytail, and she had the shirttails of that plaid shirt—clearly worn for his benefit—tied at her waist. The white tee she had on under it wasn't very practical for picking, but at least she'd worn jeans. Jeans that clung to her like a second skin, but they were jeans. And she had on green canvas sneakers. Not the most protective things in the world, but at least they weren't high heels. Although those skintight jeans would look damn good with stilettos…

He sat up straight and chased that thought clear out of his mind. Bad enough the woman made him spill his guts about his past and his family. He did *not* need to keep having these fantasies about her. He had to remember two things about Brittany: she was only in Gallant Lake temporarily, and she was up to something with this "client" of hers and his mysterious plans for a business on Nate's Main Street.

He turned the van onto a dirt driveway that led up a hill through a stand of trees. The Kennedy farm had been at the top of this little rise for well over a hundred years, but no one had lived there for the past twenty.

"Uh…please tell me you don't expect me to go in there. This place is straight out of a horror movie." Brittany stared through the windshield at the large farmhouse, with its peeling white paint and tilting front porch. Behind it was an even larger barn, the ancient bare wood making it look like it had grown right out of the ground in that spot. It had a slight lean to it, but Nate had checked it out a month ago with his architect friend, Asher. They'd deemed it structurally sound. At least sound enough for one or two people to explore gently.

The yard had vanished long ago under a tangle of weeds and scrub brush, making the place look creepier than it really was. Nate opened his door as he answered Brittany.

"As far as I know, there have been no murders up here, or paranormal activity of any kind. It's just an old farm that got left behind by the family after the owner passed. Walt Kennedy called himself a collector, but he was a borderline hoarder after he got in his eighties. There's a ton of stuff in the house and barn, and some sections are like time capsules from the past."

She stared at him, and a smile played at the corner of her mouth. "You turn into an excited little kid at these places, Nate. I've never seen anyone more excited about dirty old stuff as you are." She opened her door. "If I see one mouse or any other nasty critter in there, I'm gone."

"Don't worry about that." They walked toward the house. He was careful not to tell her it wouldn't happen, because he'd seen signs of mice in the house and heard some rustling. He knew they were in the barn, along with a boatload of spiders and bats and other stuff she didn't need to know about.

"And it's okay for us to just walk in this house with no one here?"

He held up a key. "We're not trespassing. I have permission from Walt Kennedy's daughter. She and I agreed that I could pick through and make her an offer for anything I was interested in. I've been here a couple times already, but there are so many boxes to dig through."

They started in the parlor at the front of the house. There was room to move around, but every surface had piles of boxes and random items on it. Old magazines, toys, porcelain pieces, glassware… It was almost overwhelming. He gave Brittany instructions to let him know about anything she thought might be interesting. Sometimes a stack of magazines in a box could be covering something like a Wedgwood serving platter.

There wasn't a lot of conversation as they dived in. He was sure she was still digesting the life story he'd shared. He was still digesting it, too. Grandpa had been friends with Walt Kennedy. They used to hunt and fish together. It was Walt who got Grandpa started on picking fifty years ago, but Nate's grandfather had always been more selective about what he acquired. Walt seemed to grab whatever caught his eye. He was a big fan of buying boxes of stuff without knowing what was in them. Sometimes the gamble paid off, but most of the time he ended up with boxes like those in the parlor—completely random and mostly valueless junk.

They went upstairs next, to check out the bedrooms. That was the first time in the house that he saw Brittany looking anything other than slightly disgusted. Downstairs she'd been pulling things out of boxes with the very tips of her fingers, holding them at arm's length to avoid getting dirty. But as soon as she saw the heavily carved bed, her eyes lit up. The headboard stood over seven feet tall, made of walnut and maple. It rose in the center to a crown of carved decoration and a finial that resembled an ornate fleur-de-lis. The sturdy posts had round carved finials, and the footboard was lower but had a carved medallion that matched the headboard.

Brittany was no longer afraid of dust. She wiped it off the carving on the headboard with her hand, wiping her hand off on the old bedspread, which was probably just as dirty as the headboard was. But Nate didn't say anything. He was having too much fun watching the excitement in her eyes. He was witnessing the birth of a picker. That spark of appreciation for something handmade and very old. He'd seen that look before, but it was a lot more special when it was Brittany involved.

He walked over to her. "From what I've heard, that bed was made from the wood of trees cut down right on this farm, by one of the Kennedy ancestors. It's been in this room since the day it was built."

"It's beautiful. How old do you think it is?"

He pointed to the trim work on the headboard. "That cathedral window design tells me it's from the late 1800s. It's too bad it's so small… I doubt this is even a full-size bed by today's standards. Probably takes a three-quarter mattress, which is custom."

She frowned at the bedding. "But couldn't you

have someone add to it to make it full-size? Or maybe even queen?"

He recoiled as if she'd suggested burning it. "Add on? You mean nail new wood onto an antique just to make it fit some modern aesthetic? The purpose of finding antiques is to preserve them. That would be criminal, Brittany."

She arched a brow. "More criminal than leaving it unused in a falling-down house where no one will ever be able to appreciate it?"

Nate scowled. She had a point, damn it. "Someone could use it at this size as a child's bed or something. I'm not saying it should be neglected, but…"

"Does this look like a child's bed to you? Besides, a child would probably end up carving their name in the wood or something. I'd *love* to have a bed like this." She ran her hand down the bedpost. "But you're right. It's too small as is."

They poked around the rest of the bedroom. The dressing table was clearly built at the same time as the bed, with an arched mirror that tilted in the frame, and small decorative shelves for knickknacks. A tall dresser was slightly more recent than the other pieces, but had been finished to match. It was a nice set, but Nate had no room to store or display something that large. If he could figure out how to buy Stella's shop next door to his, he could put antiques over there, and then he could move more than just smalls.

Brittany kept glancing back to the bed as they searched through drawers and boxes. They found a hat pin in one small drawer with a gold glass bead at the top, and she held it up.

"This would be perfect in the hat-pin holder in your store!"

"It would. Add it to the crate." He'd brought an old wooden crate from downstairs to put items in. He'd talk to Blanche Kennedy tomorrow and send photos and values for what he'd picked, and hopefully come to a price they could agree on. Brittany found a couple of lacy doilies that she declared she *had* to have. He explained they'd been handmade, in a craft known as tatting. She held the pieces up to examine the fine threadwork involved.

"These will look so pretty on my nightstands at home. They'll bring a little character to the room. And they'll remind me of the bed I can't have because I'd have to commit a crime to make it usable." She winked at him to let him know she was teasing, but he didn't miss the desire in her eyes when she looked back to the bed. Maybe... No. Altering an antique *would* be a crime. No self-respecting picker would even think of it. But then again, the bed was sitting up here in a vacant house, where no one was appreciating it. He snapped a few photos on his phone when Brittany wasn't looking. It wouldn't hurt to toss an offer to Blanche and see what happened.

Once they'd filled two crates with smalls he could

carry to the van, they locked up the house. The sun was settling lower in the sky, but it was still light enough to do some barn exploring. Nate thought he'd seen an old dentist chair in there that would be a great conversation piece in the store. And there was a stack of old advertising signs, even some old neon ones, against the back wall. Signs were always great sellers.

Brittany hung back after he slid the big doors open. There were two ancient farm tractors in there, probably valuable to the right collector, but way out of Nate's wheelhouse. A few antique cars, up on blocks and coated with decades of dirt and neglect, sat behind the tractors. Nate took a few photos and sent them to his buddy Wyatt, who had a commercial garage and restored cars like that. Maybe he could broker a deal between Wyatt and Blanche for the whole bunch. He looked up at the old rafters in the barn, where he could see pinholes of daylight through the roof. It would be a shame to leave the vehicles in here to rot.

Brittany cautiously followed him as he worked his way deeper into the barn.

"All this needs to complete the serial-killer vibe is a bunch of chain saws and meat hooks hanging from the rafters." She froze as something scampered across the loft floor above them. "Please tell me that was a cute kitty cat."

"It's possible," he said, turning his head away to hide his grin. "Or a squirrel. Or a raccoon. Or a rat."

She made a strangled sound, then smacked his shoulder. "You take that back right now, Nate Thomas. If there are rats in this place, I'll be waiting for you in the van."

"Relax. This place is probably a squirrel metropolis, and squirrels are harmless." That was all true. He also knew there had to be barn rats in here, but hopefully they'd stay hidden.

Her eyes narrowed to slits, but she stuck close as they went to the back wall. The air was stuffy and stale in there, and the old straw still scattered on the floor didn't help. He probably should have grabbed a couple of dust masks from the glove box in the van, but he'd been too lost in his thoughts to remember them. He'd make this quick—his primary interest was the old gas sign he'd spotted back there with the bright red Pegasus on it.

He slid a few signs to the side to expose it. Even Brittany was impressed.

"Wow, that Pegasus is gorgeous! That would look so cool hanging on a wall somewhere. And it looks in good condition…no holes, not much rust…" She stepped forward to touch it. She'd been paying more attention to his talks about antiques than he'd thought. He tipped the sign forward to show her it was two-sided. That was when all hell broke loose.

A huge barn spider, complete with a grossly bulbous belly, crawled up the sign behind the one they were looking at. But it didn't matter where it was once Brittany spied it. She let out a scream and jumped backward. He let go of the signs and reached to steady her. When the signs slammed against the wall, two small mice bolted out and ran right across the toe of her bright green tennis shoes.

While he started to laugh, Brittany's screams amped up to the earsplitting level, and she pulled away from him, turning for the door. Instead of following the same path they'd used coming in, weaving between the old cars, she went to the far side of one of the old posts—that had once been a tree trunk— holding up the beams overhead. And she ran smack into a thick wall of cobweb spanning the distance between one column and the next.

She was in an absolute panic now, frantically swinging at the cobweb to get it off her and making a keening sound of terror. He was afraid she'd hurt herself tripping over all the farm equipment between her and the doors. The old plows and menacing hay rakes could cause serious damage if she fell on them. He grabbed her arm firmly enough to pull her back. She couldn't seem to decide if she was more afraid of him or the webs hanging on her head, so she swung wildly at both. He pulled her in close and embraced her, just to pin her arms to her sides.

"Stop!" His voice was sharp enough to break through her panic. "I've got you. You're okay."

"Get me out. Please get me out…" Her voice broke.

"I will. I promise. But you have to listen to me so you don't hurt yourself." He nudged her toward the cars. As soon as her hands were free, she started clawing at the cobweb again. He took her hands in his and led her outside, where she started doing the same thing, wiping her head and chest over and over.

"Is it on me? Is it on me? Oh, my God…is that thing *on* me?" Before he could react, she'd untied the cotton shirt and flung it to the ground. She grabbed the hem of the white tee and yanked it over her head, tossing it as far as she could. And there she was, wearing only a skimpy white bra and her jeans. Her hands swept up and down her body. When she reached behind her as if to unhook her bra, he finally broke out of his shocked trance.

"Whoa, whoa. Hang on. Don't do that." As much as he'd like to see her topless, this wasn't the way. Or the time. Or the place. "You're okay. I promise."

"But what if it got inside my clothes? Ugh. I'm burning those shirts." She slapped her hands to her head. "Is it in my hair? Can you see it?"

"See *what*? The mice? They're long gone…"

"No! The spider!"

"The one from the signs? The way I dropped those things, he's probably a pancake, Britt."

"But what if he had cousins? That spiderweb was huge! If there was a spider in it, it might be on me…"

Her hands hadn't stopped moving over her skin, over her hair, down her pant legs. It was all very… distracting. He cleared his throat, trying to think of anything but the fact that she was standing there in her bra. Her tiny, sheer bra with the lace trim and a little bow right between…

Look away! Look away!

He turned to the side, but fear was still pulsating from her and he had to address it. Steeling himself, he turned back and took her hands again.

"Brittany, stop." He reached up and plucked a clump of dusty gray web from her ponytail and showed it to her. "Look how filthy this is."

"Is that supposed to make me feel better? That I just covered myself in a *filthy* cobweb?"

"Well, it *should* make you feel better. This level of dirt tells me this web has been in there for years. Which means its creator is probably long gone." He knew some spiders could actually live that long. But he was smart enough to know she didn't need to hear it. And this web looked very unused. "I know it's gross, but I think you're safe." And nearly naked.

She took a shaky breath. "Can you check? I mean… my hair…"

"Turn around." She did, giving him a break from trying not to look at her chest. Mind you, her bare back was sexy, too, but not as provocative as her lovely breasts pushing against the thin white material of her bra. He wiped the top of her head, picking off any remnants of the cobweb. He pulled the tie from her ponytail, combing his fingers through her silky long hair. Then he stepped back to inspect her from behind. There was no place for a spider of any size to hide, between all the bare skin and the tight denim. Nate's denim got a little tighter, too, as he stood there admiring her. *Inspecting* her. That was all he was doing. He just had to ignore the tawny-brown hair tumbling between her shoulder blades, not quite reaching the spot where that bra connected in the middle of her back. He was about to back up even farther when she turned to face him. *Not helping.*

She'd apparently calmed enough to realize she was nearly topless, since her arms were crossed over her breasts, and some color had returned high on her cheeks. "Anything?"

He shook his head. "You're good."

Her eyes were clouded. "Could you…um…check my T-shirt?"

Thankful for the chance to look anywhere but at her, he scooped up the tee, shaking it hard before turning it right side out and shaking it again. Before he could give her the all clear, she grabbed it from his hands and tugged it on. She flipped her now-loose hair out from the shirt, fanning it across her shoulders.

"I can't believe I yanked my clothes off in front of you. I'm…sorry. I was so freaked out…"

"You think?" He grinned, more relieved than

sorry that she was covered again. It was easier to look in her eyes now. "I was afraid you were going to impale yourself on the farm tools in there." He picked up her plaid shirt from the ground and shook it out, too. He flipped it over and checked it before handing it back to her.

She shrugged it on, stepping toward him while still looking down to tie the shirttails together. Her hands were shaking, and before he knew what was happening, Nate took the shirt and started to tie it. They were standing close now, and his knuckles brushed the white tee. He could feel her stomach beneath it. Did she just tremble?

She looked up through her long lashes. A tiny dimple appeared as she struggled not to smile and failed. Her hand rested on his arm, then slid up to his biceps, which tightened of their own accord. Or maybe because her touch made his body feel like it was being tased. Her pupils went wide and dark, and watching that happen from this close sent a surge of heat through his veins.

How did his hand get to the side of her face, where she leaned into his palm? Were they puppets being controlled by unseen strings, pulling them together and tangling around them? What else could explain the fact that her chest was pressed against his now, and her lips were right there. Just an inch from his, because he'd lowered his head toward her. Why had…? Ah, who gave a damn why or what or how?

All he cared about was her arm sliding around his neck. Her fingers in his hair. His hand against her back, magically working its way under both shirts so he could feel her warm, soft skin. The feel of her mouth against his, featherlight and cautious at first. He slid his lips across hers, back and forth, back and forth. And then she pushed up onto her toes and forced solid contact.

The match was lit. He cupped the back of her head and kissed her, throwing caution and feathers right out the window. If he was going to do something this crazy, he may as well do it big. Her lips parted for him and he went in, all thoughts ceasing as he focused only on sensation.

Chapter Eight

Brittany thought her heart might just pound its way right out of her chest as Nate got serious about kissing her. He turned his head for better access and plunged inside her mouth. His hand flattened against the small of her back, skin to skin. Pulling her against him. Was that…was that an erection she was bumping up against? So much for mild-mannered Nate Thomas.

It was clear neither of them had planned this kiss. She'd had her freak-out. And had been mortified to realize she'd ripped off her clothes right in front of him. And he'd been so calm about it all, like women stripped for him every day. The calm was what she expected from the man. But this? This hard, deep kiss that made her toes curl? Not expected at all.

This was a man who was kissing her like she was one of those treasures he talked about finding. Like she was *his*.

And just like that, it was over. He set her back, away from him, staring at her with…confusion? Desire? Regret? Oh, that last one hurt. What would make him regret a kiss that good?

"Nate…"

"I'm sorry." He released her and turned away, cupping his hands on the back of his head. "I shouldn't have done that. *We* shouldn't have done that. If I took advantage…"

"Nate, I was just as much a participant as you were."

He spun, a look of disbelief on his face. "But why?"

"I…" Her mind went blank on how to answer that question. "Why *what*? We had a moment, and we went for it."

"We shouldn't have."

Her shoulders tensed. He was spoiling the moment with all of his angst. The fact that he was right made her even more irritated. They shouldn't have kissed. Until she could figure out what was happening with Conrad's plans for Gallant Lake, she needed to be careful. Getting personally involved with a potential rival—the president of the preservation society, for heaven's sake—was a bad idea. Even if it was a damn good kiss.

"Look, it was just a kiss. I'm a big girl, Nate. I know you didn't want to get involved." He started to speak, but she waved him off. "But you can relax. I'm not expecting us to go steady or anything." She headed toward the van, her emotions a jumble of anger and desire. "You know what? Never mind. You're right. We *shouldn't* have. Let's get out of this creepy-ass place."

They drove back to the lake in silence. It wasn't the comfortable silence like they had after going to the llama farm. This was tense and heavy. He pulled up to her cabin, then sat back, staring straight ahead.

"I want to be clear about one thing, Brittany. I enjoyed that kiss. A lot. So don't think that's what this is about. I'm just not a…" His fingers drummed against the steering wheel. "I'm not a casual relationship sort of guy. If I kiss a woman, it means I'm serious, and…"

She yanked at the door handle. Hard.

"And you can't see yourself getting serious about a woman like me, right?"

She knew she sounded petulant, but she was *feeling* petulant, damn it.

Nate let out a sigh. "That is not what I said. Or meant. It shouldn't surprise you to hear I'm kind of an old-fashioned guy. We barely know each other.

You're in town for a few weeks, and you're involved in some shady-sounding business deal…"

She got out of the van, hiding her hurt from him. She'd had people treating her like someone shady her whole life. Especially when she, Mom and Ellie had been scraping by on the streets. She'd hated the distrust in people's eyes when she'd ask for a few dollars to buy a couple of burgers with so she and Ellie wouldn't go hungry. Even if they gave her something, it was usually with a comment about not spending it on drugs or booze. As if her fifteen-year-old self would *ever* do that.

"Thanks for the day, Nate." Her voice was flat. "See you around."

He called her name, but she walked to the cabin without looking back. She didn't want him to see the tears in her eyes. She didn't want him to know how much she cared about what he thought of her. Because she shouldn't care. This stab of pain was proof of it.

Her sister knew something was wrong as soon as Brittany called her the next morning. She'd just left Nora's coffee shop and made sure to walk *away* from the hardware store. She tried to deflect Ellie's questions, but it was pointless.

"There's this guy…"

"Oh, my God. A *guy*?" Ellie laughed. "Tell me everything. Right now."

"Turns out there's nothing to tell. I think I was

more…curious…than anything, but then we had this weird moment and kissed, and it was…amazing." She smiled a greeting at the police chief, Dan Adams, as he passed her on the sidewalk. "But he doesn't do *casual*, so he ended it before it ever got started." She took a deep breath. "And that's a good thing. This guy is a settle-down-and-start-a-family type, and you know better than anyone that's…not for me."

"I know no such thing. You deserve to find love, Britt-Britt."

She scoffed, walking by Mack Wallace, who was unlocking the front door to her liquor store. "Who said anything about *love*? I was just looking for a little fun, but Nate was one kiss and done."

Ellie laughed. "Nice rhyme, sis!"

"Yeah, ha ha." She shook her head, trying to shake off Nate's kiss, too. "It's no big deal. I'll just move on. I always do."

"Someday you're gonna get tired of all that movin' on, sis."

Someday is already here.

"Who, me? I'm a rolling stone, kiddo. I'll give you a call later, okay?"

She walked on, turning down a side street and walking down sidewalks lined with charming older homes. Some were Victorian, but most were sturdy square houses like Nate's, solid and practical. They had sharply-pitched roofs to handle the winter snow-fall. The yards were tidy, and most had flowers all around. It was a nice town. She could understand why Nate wanted to preserve it.

She couldn't keep the man out of her head, so she tried to change her focus. Instead of thinking about The Kiss, she tried to come up with a way to keep the hardware store intact and still deliver Conrad what he wanted. Maybe she could convince him to scale back the number of condos. Or bump them to the east of Nate's store, extending farther that direction instead of being centered in downtown. She walked back to Main Street and looked at the area. There was an old firehouse there that was vacant.

It was a cool place, part of the town's history, and distinctive with the arched windows on the old wood doors, now sealed shut. The building would make a fun office or storefront. And it was for sale. She jotted down the number. It would be a shame to see it demolished for condos, but whoever bought it might tear it down anyway. She snapped a few photos and took some information on other nearby properties.

She was headed back to her car when she heard Mack calling her name. The door to the liquor store had been propped open, probably to let the fresh air in. She stepped inside and saw Mack ringing up a sale for Stella. The older woman gave her a wink as she left, honoring their little secret of an offer on Stella's building. It was still just a verbal agreement until she had everyone lined up, but it was a step in the right direction. For Conrad, at least.

Mack was giving her the strangest look from behind the counter. Both amused and curious.

Brittany looked down at her clothes, wondering if
she had her shirt on inside out or something. Nope,
everything looked tidy, just the way she liked it.

"What are you grinning at?"

"Oh…nothing." Mack came around the counter.
"Just wondering if I heard right earlier."

Brittany went still. Had rumors started about her
making offers on properties? She swallowed hard.

"What did you hear?"

"I hate to admit to eavesdropping, but I couldn't
help overhearing when you walked by earlier. I could
swear I heard you on the phone using the words *Nate*
and *kiss* in the same sentence."

Brittany's face burned. She thought nothing of
strolling city streets while on the phone, with strangers pressing in all around her. But that didn't happen
in Gallant Lake. Not a chance. One lousy phone call
on a quiet weekday morning, and naturally it was
overheard by someone who not only knew her, but
also didn't mind asking her about it directly.

Mack held her hands up. "Hey, I didn't mean to
put you on the spot…" Brittany gave her a look, and
Mack laughed. "Okay, I meant to put you on a *little*
spot. But if you don't want to talk about it, it's cool.
I just want to say Nate's about as good as a man can
get. I went to school with him, and he's true blue,
honorable, all that Scout stuff." She grinned. "And

he's got that hot nerd look down to a T. Don't let the flannel and plaid scare you off."

"I wasn't the one who got scared off." Brittany shrugged. "But it's honestly for the best. He said he doesn't do casual, and I'm not staying, so…"

"He wasn't lying. I've never known him to just hook up with anyone. He's dated a few women, but it's been a while. Maybe because of his parents' divorce… I don't know."

Brittany couldn't resist asking, even if it was going to prove her interest. "Divorced? What happened?"

Mack looked out the window, as if making sure no one was listening, which was ironic, considering how this conversation had started. She gestured for Brittany to follow her to the back of the store, where wine-tasting area was set up. They sat at a café table.

"Nate's dad had a bad gambling problem."

Brittany nodded. "He mentioned his father liked Atlantic City."

Mack's brows rose. "Wow. He very rarely talks about it. His dad had always been a little edgy. He resented the store. Fought with Nate's grandfather all the time. Did some drinking. But it was the gambling that did him in." She sat back, and her expression turned sad. "It destroyed his marriage. He took out a loan against the store to cover his debts, and they almost lost the place. Nate and his grandfather really never forgave him. I think Nate just got that mortgage paid off a few years ago."

She digested that news. No wonder he was so resentful of change. His dad wanted to change everything and blew up Nate's whole world.

"Where's his dad now?"

Mack shook her head. "He passed away about ten years ago."

"His mom?"

"Oh, she's fine. She remarried and lives in Florida with her husband and Nate's half sister." Mack's head tilted. "Now it's your turn to talk. How did you end up kissing our Nate?"

Our Nate. This town loved Nate as much as he loved the town. They were permanently entwined. She told Mack about the spiderweb and the kiss.

"Wait a minute. He took you *picking* with him? And then he told you about his dad? And saw you half-naked and then *kissed* you? Girl, you're already more than casual. What made him pull away?"

"Like I said, I'm not staying here. We have nothing in common. He was right to pull the plug."

"But you wish he hadn't."

She opened her mouth to deny it but couldn't.

"It stung a little."

Mack reached over and squeezed her hand. "Don't give up on him if that's what you really want."

Brittany chuckled. "I don't know what I'd do with him if I caught him. But I'm fine, Mack. Do me a favor and keep this on the down low, okay? I'd hate to embarrass him with rumors."

"Sure thing." Brittany was almost to the door when Mack called out. "Hey, did you see the forecast for this weekend? They say we could get some wild storms. If you get nervous about that old cabin floating away, just give Dan and me a call. You're welcome to stay at our place."

Brittany thanked her for the offer and headed back to the cabin, unconcerned about the weather. A little rain wasn't going to worry her. She was more concerned with coming up with a viable proposal for Conrad. Her preference was to reduce the footprint of the condos, if she could talk him into it. Now that she was getting to know more people in town, she knew her friends, like Nora, Mack and Mel, would probably be horrified to see modern condos built right across the street from their businesses. She reminded herself that the condos would bring more customers for those businesses. But it would drastically change the face of Gallant Lake, even if they didn't use Nate's Hardware. It would be small consolation for him to keep his store but lose "his" town.

Because of her.

The storm hit exactly when forecast—in the wee hours of the morning. Nate had been checking his weather app since early the day before. That was when the local meteorologist in White Plains had declared a Storm Team Weather Watch Stay Alert Day or whatever they called it. The channel liked to do that at the least hint of bad weather, but this one sounded legit. A strong weather system was roaring up from the Ohio Valley, gathering energy as it came. They figured when that cold front hit the hot, humid air in New York, things could get dicey, with high winds and dangerous lightning.

He'd tried to say something to Brittany about it when he saw her out walking that afternoon, with the ragtag little stray trotting at her side. He remembered the way she'd flinched at every roll of thunder that very first day she stumbled into his store and thought she might want to know. But she must have still been steamed about him putting a stop to that kiss a week ago, because she made a point to level him with her coolest gaze. Check that…make that her *iciest* gaze. And that woman could do icy really well.

"Seriously, Nate? Just because I freaked out after walking into the world's largest spiderweb doesn't mean I need a babysitter for a rainstorm." Yeah, her pride had been pricked, and she was making her independence known. So be it. She was right. She was a grown woman who'd made it very clear she did *not* want his help. Or his kisses.

He heard the first rumbles of thunder in the distance around one o'clock in the morning. It was still a long way off, but the low grumbling sound was nearly constant, boom after boom after boom, with the echoes rolling over each other between the mountains. It sounded angry. He sat up and opened the radar app on his phone. *Yikes.* A long, sharp blob of red and purple on the screen was marching toward Gallant Lake, with multiple little lightning bolts popping all over the front line. Several colored triangles overlaid the radar, indicating locations of hail, high winds, severe storm warnings and even a tornado watch that covered most of the Catskills. Not good.

He closed the bedroom windows and headed out to take care of the rest of the house. His gray tabby cat, Pepper, zigzagged around his feet, meowing loudly. The cat probably sensed the drop in air pressure. Nate closed the windows in the kitchen and dining room. The storm was getting louder with every step he took, the night sky flickering nonstop with light. By the time he reached the living room windows facing the lake, it was raining hard and the wind was starting to gust. He thought of Brittany, then dismissed it. Her little cabin was sturdy. Probably. He smiled as he picked up his cat. For sure with that metal roof, she was going to have a noisy night.

Right on cue, hailstones started hitting the side of his house, and the power flickered and went out. Once the house went pitch-black, Pepper had no interest in being held. Since Nate had no interest in being shredded by those claws, he let the cat jump to the back of the sofa, thunder rattling the pictures on the wall. Within a minute the big generator outside fired up and the electric box switched over with a clunking sound. *Let there be light.* He'd bought the generator and had it hooked up to his propane tank a few years back, after an ice storm had left much of the town without power for days. It didn't come on often, but he was glad for it tonight. It would keep the lights, fans and appliances going.

The storm was right overhead now, and it was a doozy. Bad enough that Nate wondered how downtown and the store were making out. The lake looked wild whenever the lightning lit it up, which meant the boardwalk was at risk, too. *Nah.* He'd built that sturdy enough to survive a summer storm, even a crazy one like this. But it *was* intense—loud and bright, the lightning looking like strobe lights outside the windows. Aware of the cat still hiding under the sofa, he sat in his grandfather's oversize rocking chair and watched the show. At one point the wind started howling so loudly that he moved the chair back from the windows, just in case. He was pretty sure some of the crashing sounds he heard out there were limbs, and possibly even trees, coming down. He thought again of Brittany, and now the thought left him unsettled. This was no "rainstorm."

This was a once-in-a-decade sort of storm, and suddenly he wasn't sure exactly *how* sturdy those old camps really were. He got up and grabbed his heavy flashlight and rain slicker, then started lacing up his boots. As soon as things let up out there, he'd go check on her. Just as a good neighbor. To make sure things were okay. That *she* was okay. But there was nothing he could do right now, while the rain still lashed at the windows and the thunder sounded like someone was throwing sticks of dynamite around out there.

Brittany was pretty sure this was what the end of the world sounded like. The cottage shuddered in the wind. The rain and hail were making a hellish amount of noise on the metal roof. Joey had woken her not long ago, pawing at her ribs and whining. Brittany had blinked and rolled over, muttering at the dog and hoping to get back to sleep. Then the room erupted in a flash of blinding blue-yellow light, followed almost instantly by an explosion so loud she thought the propane tank outside may have blown up. Joey bolted off the bed, with Brittany right behind him. She dashed around the house in her pajama shorts and cami, struggling to close windows against the wind that came out of nowhere, creating horizontal rain. Joey was right at her heels, barking in an even more elevated pitch than usual. He was not helping her nerves.

There are storms headed this way tonight. You might want...

She'd cut Nate off that afternoon before he could finish offering whatever help or advice he was going to offer. He was such a fuddy-duddy, worrying about weather as if she was a child who couldn't handle a summer storm. As if that stupid kiss—the one she couldn't stop dreaming about—meant he had a right to offer her advice. Like they were in a relationship or something.

As the storm increased in intensity, she started to wonder. Maybe…just maybe…she should have listened to him. But then again…she had it under control. Sure, it was loud, but loud couldn't hurt you, right? Just as she closed the small window over the sink, congratulating herself for making the cottage watertight, she noticed water seeping under the closed windows in the living room. Brittany grabbed some towels from on top of the washing machine and dashed toward the windows to stop the leak.

She was halfway across the room when the lights went out. If she thought the lightning was bright before, it was blinding when it cut through the pitch darkness. It was also nearly nonstop, which at least allowed her to pick her way over to the windows in the light, rolling up the towels and lining the windowsills with them.

Okay. This was fine. It was storming, but that was outdoors, and she was inside. Even Joey seemed to sense safety, because he stopped barking for a moment. The silence was a blessing, and Brittany took in a steadying breath. She was just letting it out slowly when the front door blew open with a crash, hitting the side table and sending a glass bowl to the floor. Her own scream drowned out Joey's hysterical barking. Brittany ran to close the door, thankful she'd slipped on those flip-flops that Nate had given her in the hardware store.

She got the door closed, but the wind was so strong that it wouldn't stay latched, so she turned and put her back against it, bracing her legs to hold it shut. Was this a tornado? Was she about to go to Oz? One thing was certain—this shack wouldn't be able to sustain much more wind like this. She couldn't even go to a safe place, if there was such a thing in this thing, because if she moved, the door would open and bring the storm inside. Something was rattling and banging overhead… The roof? Was she going to *die* in this rustic fish camp in a little town no one had ever heard of? The door pushed against her back, like some monster was trying to force its way in. Surely, this wouldn't last much longer. There were frightening noises outside…an unearthly ripping sound, like something large being torn apart, then an enormous crash that shook the house. How much longer was this going to last?

It seemed like forever that she stood there, holding the door closed by sheer willpower, listening to Joey lose his mind barking while flashes of light flickered past the windows. But the storm, as all storms did, eventually began to settle. The thunder was farther away, slower to come after the flashes of lightning. The roar of rain on the roof began to level off, and finally, mercifully, the wind settled from hurricane-force to just plain windy. She stayed against the door, partly out of fear it might still whip open, and partly because less frequent lightning meant less frequent *light*. The cabin was pitch-dark between strikes. There was an old jarred candle in the kitchen, but were there matches anywhere? A flashlight? Oh… her phone. Where was it? She leaned her head back against the door. Her phone was all the way in the bedroom, still attached to a useless charger. She took another deep breath, pulling her shoulders up and giving herself a quick pep talk. Surely, she could get in there without tripping over anything.

She did, with Joey's help. The dog kept dashing in front of her, so she'd listen to his nails clicking on the wood floor and follow the sound. It may have been a zigzagging path, but she didn't fall. She grabbed her phone, turned on the flashlight and set it on the bed pointing up. Her striped Brooks Brothers shirt hung on the bedpost, and she shrugged it on like a robe. The tails hung down over her pajama shorts, but who cared? She just wanted to step outside and make sure the cottage was still in one piece. Not to mention her rental car. Very practical of her. Very mature. Not the actions of a woman who'd just faced down death.

She looked down at Joey and swallowed hard, forcing a smile on her face. For the dog's sake, of course. "We got this, right? Totally. We got this."

They were almost back to the front door when there was a banging sound and the door flew open. As if that wasn't frightening enough, a quick flash of lightning showed the outline of a man in the doorway. Once again she and Joey made their noise in unison. Joey charging forward, snarling and barking, and Brittany... She opened her mouth to scream, but never heard it before everything went dark and silent.

"Brittany? Brittany? Wake up, girl."

A familiar voice came from over her head. How did someone get over her head? And why couldn't she see them? Oh...she had to open her eyes first. *Eh, maybe later.* Right now she felt very comfortable in this person's arms. She wasn't alone anymore, the storm was over and she was safe. She felt safer than she had in years. That was weird. Oh, there was that voice again.

"Brittany?" A hand gently moved over her hair, as if checking for damage. "Are you hurt? Come on—open those eyes and yell at me so I know you're okay."

Nate? Was that *Nate*? Her eyes flew open, but she was still disoriented. A lantern of some sort was sitting on the floor, throwing odd shadows around the cottage. She and Nate were on the floor, too. And he was holding her against his chest. She was so confused. Had the storm been a bad dream? But what was Nate doing here? Maybe *this* was the dream.

She took a few deep, quick breaths and her voice returned.

"What happened?"

"There was a storm…"

Irritation rushed up inside her. She didn't like being at a disadvantage like this. She pushed away from him and sat up.

"I *know* there was a storm. What are *you* doing here? Why are we…?" She gestured between them. And there it was—the tiniest of quirks at the corner of his mouth. Nate Thomas's perpetual amusement with her.

"I came to check on you and apparently scared the daylights out of you. You fainted."

"I did *not*." There was no way that she just *fainted* in front of Nate Thomas.

His mouth slid into a real smile now. "I'm afraid you did. It was my fault, though. I probably looked like Freddy Krueger standing in the doorway. Sorry." He reached out and smoothed her hair. He *smoothed* her hair! She swatted his hand away, but his smile didn't budge. "I take it you didn't hurt yourself, then?"

"No." Her voice cracked. Her anger refused to stay in place. She just didn't have the energy to sustain it. "I'm not hurt. I…I can't believe I did that. I've never fainted in my life." She blinked, rubbing her face with her shaking hands. The adrenaline rush was wearing off, chased by exhaustion. "The door wouldn't stay shut…the wind… I had to lean on it to hold it shut the whole time…" She looked up at him. "What the hell *was* that? A tornado?"

"I don't think so, but it's too soon and too dark to tell. It seemed more like straight-line winds, but it was wilder than anything I've seen in years." He looked toward the door. "If you were standing at that door the whole time, you got lucky. That big maple just missed hitting you—it came down right outside that side of the cabin."

That must have been the horrible sound she'd heard in the storm. The death throes of that huge tree. She looked around the room, moving to get up, her heart racing.

"Where's Joey? You didn't let him out, did you?"

Nate put his hand on her arm to stop her from standing, then gave a short, sharp whistle through his teeth. Joey came out from behind the sofa, looking sheepish, but his tail was wagging. He burrowed into Brittany's arms, and she buried her face in his scraggly fur.

"What are you, the animal whisperer?"

He shrugged, but there was an odd look in his eye as he watched her snuggle the dog.

"I'd like to claim credit, but your dog would never leave here without you."

"He's not my dog." The response was fast. Automatic. Emphatic. Just like her denial of fainting. Then Joey licked her face. Nate shook his head.

"Yeah, okay."

Her brain was still short-circuiting a little. She couldn't focus when she looked into Nate's warm eyes. It must be because of the whole fainting thing. It had nothing to do with the crazy idea in her head that she wouldn't mind if he kissed her right now. Even though she'd told him to never even think about doing that again. She blinked. *Stop thinking about kissing.*

"Uh…something was loose and banging on the roof during the storm."

He glanced up. "Might be a loose piece of metal. I'm sure Vince will be out to check on things, but I'll text him. One of the vacant cabins took a hard hit from a pine tree in one corner."

She stared at his profile as he continued looking at the ceiling. Even from this angle, in the muted light of the lantern, all of his lines were soft. Strong. Inviting.

"Why?" Oh, God, she'd blurted that out loud.

Nate looked back to her. "Why what?"

"Oh, uh…why are you here?"

He grinned, leaning back against the sofa and stretching one leg out in front of him, resting his arm on his other knee. "Do you mean existentially or just here in this cabin?"

"Ha ha. Why did you come here—" she gestured toward his wet hair and soaked clothing "—in the pouring rain? The storm wasn't even over yet."

"I'm not a fool—I waited until it was *pretty* much over. As far as why, I came to check on you and your mutt." He ruffled Joey's fur. "And now I think you two had better come back to my place."

"What? No, I'm…"

"Brittany, I have a generator. Lights. Power. Hot water. A sound roof." He stood, extending his hand to help her up. "*And* a guest room. No ulterior motives here. But first I want to check on how the rest of the town made out." He pulled out his phone and started tapping, glancing at her exposed legs. "Take the lantern and go grab some clothes. And actual shoes. It won't be safe walking out there like that."

She realized all she was wearing was her long-tailed striped shirt, pajamas and…bare skin. Her cheeks warmed, and she turned away as she heard him speak into his phone.

"Dan? Yeah, I know you're swamped. Have you been down Main Street yet?" He listened, his shoulders relaxing. "Good news. How's your place? Mack and Chloe?" He glanced at his watch, then arched a brow at Brittany when he saw she was still standing there, watching and listening over her shoulder. He gestured with his hand for her to get going. She nodded and followed the unspoken order. This was no time for her to be stubborn about being bossed around. As she got to her door, she heard him asking Dan a question. "Where do you need me?"

Chapter Nine

Nate set his chain saw on the ground and sat on a log from an enormous old oak tree that had fallen during the storm. It was now in large heavy sections, and no longer blocking the driveway. He and a crew of volunteers were at the Halcyon property, where they'd gone after clearing trees at the Gallant Lake Resort next door. Halcyon was an actual castle, on the historic register. It was also a family home to the owners of the resort, Blake and Amanda Randall. Blake sat next to him with a loud groan.

"Are we done yet? I seriously don't think my back can take much more."

Nate huffed out a short, tired laugh of understanding. Despite their differences in the past, Blake was a good guy, and an avid hiker and fisherman when he had the time. But he'd be the first to admit he was more at home behind a desk than cutting logs in the half-light of predawn. He owned a half dozen resorts in addition to his home base here in Gallant Lake and was probably worth millions. But you'd never know it right now, as Blake looked up to the stone mansion he'd brought back to life a few years ago.

He'd originally wanted to tear the place down, when Nate had led a local group who fought him in court to preserve Halcyon. Now that century-old house, and his family within it, was the most important thing in the world to Blake. And he and Nate had worked out a truce and tentative friendship after the court battles. The power was still out across the valley, so the windows of Halcyon were dark, and the pink-hued granite looked gray and blurry in the soft light. Blake clapped Nate on the back.

"Thank you for your help, especially at the resort. We couldn't afford to have access blocked for guests or emergency vehicles."

Nate nodded. "No problem. Any damage to any buildings that you know of?"

"A few leaking windows at the resort during the worst of it, when it was raining sideways. The clubhouse at the golf course had some water damage when one of the doors flew open." He glanced up at the castle with a grin. "This old place took it without flinching. My daughter was crying during the storm, but Amanda told Maddy that Halcyon would never fall." His smile deepened. "And there's the real man of the house." He waved to the tall, dark-haired teenager walking toward them. Zachary Randall was Blake's nephew, but Blake and Amanda had adopted him after his mother died. That was six years ago, when the boy had been only ten. The year Blake and Amanda had met and married.

"Mom told me to bring you guys some coffee. And she said I could help as long as I stayed with you. Is that okay?" Zach handed them both tall travel mugs steaming with hot coffee.

Blake chuckled. "In other words, you wore her down over the past—" he looked at his watch "—three hours and now she's making you *my* problem so she can get some sleep?"

In typical teen fashion, Zach fought the smile that played at the corners of his mouth. "Something like that. But she's not sleeping. She's headed to the resort to help in the kitchen. They're making breakfast for all the volunteers."

Blake's forehead furrowed in concern. Then he shrugged. "It's not like she needs my permission. She wouldn't listen anyway. What about Maddy?"

"Sleeping. Sue came up from the resort to stay with her."

"Okay, then. I guess you're with us. Where to next, Nate?"

Before he could answer, Zach jumped in. "Have you been to your store? Is Hank okay?"

"He's good. Salty as ever." Police chief Dan Adams told Nate the downtown area had fared well through the storm, but he'd stopped to check on Hank anyway, just to be sure. The hardware store was secure and dry. Hank was agitated, but otherwise seemed fine. Nate had been so relieved that he'd allowed the bird to run through his curse word repertoire three times.

"Nice, Zach," Blake said. "Ask about a *bird* before asking about people."

"Uh…sorry." The boy's cheeks flushed. "Is your house okay? Anyone hurt?"

"My place is fine, thanks." Nate took another deep drink of the coffee, eager for the caffeine to kick in. "Lots of damage in that area, though, especially down Long Point Road. No one injured that I know of."

Walking back to the house in the dark after the storm earlier, with Brittany holding his hand tightly, had been…interesting. She was carrying Joey cradled in her other arm. So many trees and limbs were down, scattered everywhere. They'd had to zigzag a few times to avoid contacting any power wires, which could have still been live and deadly. As they'd neared his end of the road, a few houses had lights shining in the windows, including his. Several of his neighbors had bought generators the same year he did.

Brittany had been silent until they got inside. Even then, she was quiet, but her mouth dropped open when she saw his house. There were a lot of antiques in there, but also a lot of open space. He liked room to breathe. Joey had dashed at Pepper the minute she set him down, but the cat held her place, hissing and batting the dog in the face. After a tense standoff, Pepper walked away without any interference from Joey. Brittany was almost swaying on her feet from exhaustion. He'd sent her to bed in one of the spare rooms, refusing to debate the matter. She needed sleep, and he needed to get out and help clean up his town. She hadn't put up much of a fight.

"Should we head to Long Point next?" Blake asked.

Nate nodded, squinting at the horizon as a sliver of sun began sliding into view. He wanted to help his neighbors. And check on his houseguest.

He spotted Brittany before they even got to his place. She was working under a blue plastic canopy at the closest intersection, where folding tables were set up and stacked with bottled water, doughnuts and three tall thermal coffee carafes. She wasn't alone. Nora Peyton and her cousin, Mel Brannigan—infant carrier wrapped across her chest—were serving coffee to volunteers and residents who weren't lucky enough to have generators to make their morning coffee. Nate waved out the window to Blake's SUV, sending him and Zach on down the road. But he stopped his van in front of the tent and hopped out.

"I thought I told you to get some sleep."

Her smile didn't falter. Neither did her wit. "I thought I told you I don't take orders well."

He declined the coffee she offered and took a water instead. He dropped his voice so no one else could hear. "Are you feeling okay?"

She hesitated, then nodded. "I'm tired, but so is everyone else. Other than that I'm good. How about you? At least I caught a couple hours' sleep before the chain saws woke me up. I saw the ladies setting up here and came to help."

Nate couldn't resist needling her. "That's pretty small-town of you, Britt. Are we starting to rub off on you?"

Her golden-brown eyes sharpened, but before she could answer, Mel interrupted. She had one arm cupped under her wee baby, even though he was securely swaddled and sound asleep.

"You leave her alone, Nate Thomas. She's fitting in just fine. She'll be one of us before you know it."

He saw a flicker of emotion cross Brittany's face. Was it possible she was liking it here? The way her eyes refused to meet his made the emotion look more like guilt. Before he could analyze it any further, Nora called out over her shoulder as she accepted more boxes of doughnuts from a woman who'd made it out of town and to a doughnut shop somewhere.

"Quit harassing the help, Nate! She has work to do, and so do you. I heard the Halls had a big tree down that hit their shed, right next door to your place." She walked over and patted Brittany's arm before taking Nate's elbow and leading him toward his van, her voice dropping and her latent Southern accent popping up. "Look, you two are adorable and all, but I need Brittany to help me deliver coffee and doughnuts to the power company crews working down on Lakeside Road. I promise I'll bring her back." They stopped by his van door. "She told me you came to get her after the storm. That was nice of you." He figured Brittany probably didn't embarrass herself by telling the *whole* story. He slid into the van, but Nora wasn't done with him. "Even if you *did* scare her so bad she passed out, you knucklehead." She winked. "Why don't you save us all a lot of stress and kiss the girl already?"

It must have been his exhaustion that lowered his filters.

"I tried that. Didn't go so well."

Nora's mouth dropped open. "With all the vibes between you two? I can't believe there was no chemistry if you kissed her."

Oh, there'd been plenty of chemistry. There'd been a whole laboratory *full* of chemistry. But she'd made her position very clear.

"She's only here on business, Nora. There's no point in starting something."

Nora grinned. "Ah…so there *was* chemistry. You just don't know what to do about it." She looked around, making sure no one was close enough to overhear. "You've been alone a long time, sweetie. There's nothing wrong with temporary, as long as you both understand what you're doing. You're both clearly jonesing for each other. My advice is just do it already." She stepped back, raising her hands in an exaggerated shrug. "But hey, what do I know?"

He left the coffee tent and joined Blake and Zach at the Halls' house, cutting up the tree and trying to salvage what was left of the shed and its contents by covering it with a large blue tarp. He'd tossed a stack of the tarps in his van when he'd stopped at the store. Not to sell, of course, but simply because people needed them.

As the sun rose and the amount of damage became more visible, Nate knew they were in for a long day on no sleep. But the work had to be done, tired or not. That was what neighbors did for neighbors. Utility crews were out, too, cutting power to lines for safety and replacing broken poles and connections. The Powells' house had the power lines ripped right off the house, but Eddie Trent, a local electrician, was already on a ladder working on repairs. Three houses over, the Blakefields were standing in front of their house, watching volunteers remove the big pine tree that was resting on their garage. From the looks of it, the cars inside were okay, but there was no way to get them out until the tree was out of the way.

He didn't get home until late afternoon, dead on his feet. He'd been on autopilot for hours, and that was no way to operate a chain saw. When he'd reached the point where he could barely lift the thing after refilling the gas tank for the third time, he knew he had to get some rest before he hurt himself or someone else. He made a quick drive to town, where power had already been restored, to make sure Hank had food. Then he returned home. The gas generator was still humming away, telling him power had *not* been restored on Long Point. With the number of utility crews he'd seen working, he figured it would be tomorrow before it came back.

The house was silent when he walked in, and for a moment he thought Brittany and Joey were gone. Then the dog lifted his head from his perch on the back of the sofa, his tail thumping on the cushion before he dropped his head and closed his eyes again. The dog was too tired to bark. To his surprise, Pepper was there on the sofa, too. She'd taken a position on the upholstered arm, probably because it offered a fast escape route. But she didn't seem too concerned, her face planted in her curled-up paws. Knowing that mutt Brittany refused to claim wouldn't be far from her side, he headed to the sofa and peeked over the back.

Sure enough, she was sound asleep there, curled

up on one end of the sofa, both end pillows under her head. Her chestnut hair, usually tamed into a knot or a ponytail, was free. It covered her face in damp waves, and he realized she must have showered when she got back from volunteering. Thinking that was a really good idea, he did the same, coming back out after his shower to coax her into her bed. *Her* bed. Not his. *Wipe that thought clean away.*

She hadn't moved while he'd been gone. She was wearing dark capri leggings and an oversize white Gallant Lake T-shirt. Was that *his* shirt? The idea sent a jolt of energy to a place on his body that had no business being energized. He took a deep breath and tried to think of something else...*anything* else. Chain saws. Doing inventory. Paying bills. Yeah, that one did it. His ill-timed arousal faded.

She'd have a crick in her neck for sure if he left her sleeping in this position. He walked around the sofa and sat next to her, resting his hand on her shoulder. She muttered something and swatted at him in slow motion.

"Come on, Britt." He kept his voice low so as not to jolt her awake. "You should go stretch out in a real bed."

Stop thinking about beds. Stop thinking about beds.

She mumbled again, sitting up with her eyes still closed, then slumping against him with all her weight.

He wasn't prepared and fell back on the sofa, with Brittany warm and sleepy against him.

"Britt, this isn't gonna work…"

She let out a soft snore, proving that it worked just fine for her. Truth be told, it was working pretty well for him, too. A cozy Brittany blanket might have been what he'd needed more than anything else. Feeling his eyes getting heavy, he stopped fighting it. He scooched back on the sofa, bringing her with him, until they were both stretched out together. The pillows were stuck on the other end, by their feet, but he didn't care. He was able to reach the blanket his mother had crocheted for him years ago, and he wadded it up as a pillow for them. Britt cooed something and burrowed into his arms.

It was a good thing he was so weary, or there'd have been something very different happening here. But that enticing thought barely flickered in the back of his mind as he closed his eyes and rested his head on hers. His body didn't need passion right now. It needed sleep.

Brittany tried to move and couldn't. She didn't really want to wake up, but she had to figure out why it felt like she was wedged in a warm, cushioned vise of some sort. Her eyes blinked open, and she struggled to focus in the dim light. She was facing the back cushions of Nate's leather sofa. Oh, yes—she remembered curling up there after her shower. The view of the lake had been so pretty through the wall of windows that she figured she'd enjoy it while her hair dried, and then she'd go to bed in his guest room and get some sleep. Obviously, from the gray light of evening setting in, she'd fallen asleep on the sofa. But… what was this warmth pressing against the length of her back? Or the weight she felt at her waist?

She turned her head and froze. Nate Thomas was sound asleep next to her. And his arm was around her waist, gripping tight even in slumber. How had *that* happened? She had a vague memory of his voice in her ear…of them stretching out together, his head resting on hers with a sigh. It had felt like a dream, but she was definitely awake now, and they were definitely spooning on his sofa.

Her forehead furrowed. She should be sitting up and shoving him to the floor. She should be telling him off for getting cozy with her while she was sleeping and defenseless. She should be stomping off to her own little cabin and leaving him in her dust. But she didn't do any of those things. Why wasn't she doing at least *one* of those things? Her eyes closed, as if that would keep her from seeing the truth.

She didn't want to give this up just yet. The feeling of being wrapped up in Nate Thomas. The scent of him, like fresh air mixed with soap. The brush of his breath on her ear. The weight of him along her body.

He took in a deeper breath behind her, rubbing his nose on her neck.

"You awake?" His voice was as rough as the rocks along the lake, as deep as the water itself.

"Yes." She barely breathed the word out loud, reluctant to have him wake up completely. He might leave her there alone if he woke, and she didn't want that. She wanted to hold on to this moment a little longer.

He stretched, pressing himself even closer, his arm tightening. A quiver of arousal shot through her. That was a bad idea, of course. But then again…

"Don't leave."

The two words came out in a rush, sounding more desperate than intended. His half-awake laughter rumbled against her.

"I'm pretty sure this is *my* house, so…"

There was no sense trying to be the levelheaded executive and arguing over semantics right now. This wasn't about their brain power. It was about the heat that had been growing between them for weeks. She wiggled against him, lightly pressing her butt against his… Oh, yeah, there he was, growing hard in response. Her belly turned to liquid lava. He growled, then sucked in a sharp breath when she did it again.

"*Damn* it, Brittany…" He gasped the words against her neck and followed them with his lips, kissing his way up to her earlobe and nipping at it with his teeth. He didn't move away. If anything, he was moving against her, sliding up and down ever so slightly. As if he didn't want to, but couldn't stop. Hard as steel. "You feel so good…"

He paused, then pulled away enough to send a chill through her.

"Stay…" she murmured, trying again to connect her body to his.

"Wait." The sleepiness was gone from his voice. He raised his head, looking down at her with eyes dark and intense. Who knew Nate Thomas could be so intense? His voice was far steadier than she could have managed right then, his tone serious. "I need you to tell me what you think is happening here. 'Cause this feels like the best freakin' dream I've ever had, but if it's not gonna continue… If you're not… I don't think my heart could handle going much further and then not…" He dropped his forehead to hers. "Jesus, Britt, I want you so bad right now."

She wanted to reach up to him, but both her arms were restricted. One held down by Nate and one pinned between her body and the sofa. So she tried to hold him with her eyes. He'd come to save her after the storm. He'd brought her to his home for safety. She'd seen pride and approval in his eyes when he saw her working with Nora and Mel. And last week he'd kissed her socks off in a dusty old barn.

"If you want me that bad, then take me, Nate."

He shook his head. "So many reasons not to, kitten."

Kitten.

"Why *kitten*?"

"Because you're cute and clever, but you also have very dangerous claws." His shoulder lifted. "And it sounds good with Britt. Britt-Kitt."

She paused, thinking of her sister's teasing Britt-Britt nickname for her. The two people she'd never managed to intimidate or fool.

"I mean it, Nate. I want this." She twisted, freeing one arm and cupping his cheek above her. "I want you."

He stared at her for a long moment, searching her face.

"I want you, too, Brittany. I swear to God I do. But… I don't know." He raked his fingers through his hair, which was already standing on end. He'd showered before lying with her. He took her hand and kissed her palm, holding it against his lips with his eyes closed, lost in thought. This was big, and she understood his conflict. But still…it wasn't *that* complicated.

"Look, I'm not asking you to marry me." Her voice sharpened. "I'm just saying let's have sex. Tonight. Not forever."

His eyes snapped open, confusion and a glint of humor in his gaze.

"So you're saying you just want a one-night stand?"

Did she really think one night would ever be enough with Nate? Maybe. Maybe all this chemistry with them was a fluke. An illusion. Once they got it out of their systems, that would be that.

"I don't know if we have to limit ourselves right off the start." She rubbed against him, making him groan again. "But sure. If it makes you feel better, a one-night stand works for me. I mean, we're both responsible adults. We're both single. No collateral damage. No commitment. It should be easy, right?"

His mouth slanted into a grin. "Just two adults having sex, huh?" His brows lowered as his smile faded. "As tempting as it might be, that's not really my thing, Britt. I'm not a one-night-stand kind of guy. Maybe we should…"

He was going to say no, and the sting of rejection hit her hard. It had taken a lot for her to put herself out there, and she'd clearly misread what was happening. The idea that she could be that wrong…or that *he* could be so obtuse as to turn her down when their bodies were ready to go. Frustration rose hot and quick. She shoved his shoulder hard with the heel of her hand, almost sending him off the edge of the sofa. Breaking some of that body connection made it easier to think.

"You know what? Never mind." Her voice rose. "I've never begged a man to make love to me in my life, and I'm sure as hell not going to start now. Get off me. I'm going back to my place." She shoved him again, and this time he wasn't able to catch himself. He windmilled for a minute before losing his balance and hitting the floor ass first. *Good.*

He landed in a seated position, so his head was still level with hers. His eyes were wide with surprise.

"Did you seriously just put me on my ass?"

"It's a good place for you since you *are* one." She sat up, tugging her shirt down. Oh, wait. That was *his* shirt. She'd grabbed it off the back of the bathroom door after her shower. It was soft and worn, and it smelled like him. Right now that scent just made her more angry at what they *weren't* going to be doing. "I'm outta here..."

"Not so fast." Nate grabbed her wrist as she started to stand, pulling her down on her knees next to him on the floor. "Damn it, Britt, lower your shields for half a minute. I know I'm waffling on you, but it has nothing to do with *you*." He cupped the back of her head and made sure she was looking at him. "I've never been a player. I'm the furthest thing from it. I'm not good at this, but I didn't mean to hurt your feelings..."

"You didn't hurt my..."

Her voice trailed off. Who was she kidding? They both knew she was lying. He pulled her closer, his hand still firmly behind her head. Their noses were almost touching, his eyes boring into her.

"I *did* hurt you, and I'm sorry. I've never been seduced like that. Whatever game I *had*, you destroyed, and I didn't know how to react." His other arm slid around her waist, nudging her sideways until she was straddling him, sitting on his thighs. "But I think I'm figuring it out now, so if you don't mind starting your seduction of me all over again, I'll try to do better."

They stared at each other, both breathing deep and slow. This was crazy, right? Then why was her heart in the same rhythm as her lungs, so steady and sure? She'd never thought of herself as a seductress, but she *was* a woman who went after what she wanted, and she wanted Nate. She leaned forward and kissed him, feeling his grip tighten around her. He gave a rough moan as his lips parted. He was letting her take the lead, but not for long. Her tongue played with his for a moment before he took over. This wasn't the sweet, sizzly hayloft kiss. This was pure heat.

His lips were demanding on hers, and she surrendered. He may not consider himself a player, but he sure *could* be one if he wanted to. He could melt a woman into a puddle of desire with his mouth. He pillaged her until she was practically whimpering. Her shoulders hit the floor, and she'd never felt him lean her back. But there he was, sliding his knee between her legs and rocking his thigh against her before lowering himself on top of her, his mouth never stopping his seductive dance.

His hands slid under her T-shirt and up her rib cage until they cupped her breasts. She pulled away for a quick gasp of air and spoke his name out loud. He dropped his head to run kisses down her neck.

"You're like gasoline, Britt, and I'm the freakin' match. I want to light you up…" He paused. "That sounds corny, right? I told you I'm bad at this." He nipped her shoulder. "Aw, hell, I don't give a damn. I want you so bad. I want you naked…"

A sharp dog bark stopped everything. Brittany's eyes flew open and she saw Joey on the sofa, staring down at them with bright eyes and a wagging tail. His expression made it clear he wanted to join whatever fun game they were playing on the floor. Before she could warn Nate, Joey leaped from the sofa to the floor, shoving his wet nose between Nate's face and Brittany's neck.

Once the initial shock wore off, they both started laughing to the point of tears. Nate sat up and lifted the dog in his arms.

"Everyone's a critic, huh? You didn't like my corny lines, either?" He grinned down at Brittany, and, instead of the moment being broken with Joey's interruption, the intensity of her desire just deepened.

Nate was in a rumpled cotton shirt with his mussed hair, holding a wiggling Joey in his arms and laughing down at her. He was hotter than ever in her eyes. When his gaze met hers, she was pretty sure she read the same thought in his eyes—maybe this was where they needed to be. Laughing and uninhibited. Not exactly familiar lovemaking territory for her. She tended to be just as intense and goal-focused in bed as she was in business. But this silly moment felt really good with Nate. Natural. Sexy.

He rose effortlessly to his feet, holding Joey in one arm while reaching down to help her up. "I think we forgot that this has been a long day for our four-legged friends, too. I'll take him outside if you'll put some food in their dishes. Leave Pepper's dish up on the counter, so Joey can't get into it." Nate flashed her a megawatt smile. "Once they're taken care of, we'll move *our* plans into the bedroom. Where there's a comfy bed." He held Joey up in front of his face and spoke directly to the dog. "And a *door.*"

Chapter Ten

Nate had a chance to steady his pulse while waiting for Joey to do his business in the yard. The sun had set, and the moon was just coming up behind Gallant Mountain. The power was still off in their neighborhood, but the hum of generators meant some of the houses, including his, had a few lights on. He looked across the water toward the resort and Halcyon, which both seemed to have electricity. That was a good sign. Hopefully, everyone would have power back by morning.

And speaking of electricity, Brittany Doyle was waiting for him inside. Waiting to have sex with him. That woman was as highly charged—and deadly—as any live electrical wire. He'd nearly bungled everything when she started flirting on the sofa. She'd caught him off guard, waking him up by moving against him just as he was dreaming of moving against her. He cringed at how much of a rube he must have seemed, acting all befuddled because a beautiful woman wanted to have sex with him. And getting an instant hard-on like some teenage virgin. No wonder she'd dumped him on his ass.

He followed the dog back to the house, locking the door. Good thing he'd come to his senses soon enough to grab Brittany and…make her laugh. That seemed to be Brittany's aphrodisiac—laughter. Which was interesting, considering she was a woman who didn't laugh all that much. Even when she was amused, she didn't often bust out into laughter. She might give a thin smile, maybe a brief chuckle if Hank did something goofy at the store.

But tonight she'd laughed with him. And not because she was amused…because she was turned on. By *him*. Go figure.

She was nowhere to be seen when he walked back into the house. For a second he worried that she'd left as she'd threatened to do earlier. Maybe she'd come to her senses and realized he was no Casanova. But no, she'd put food and water out for the dog and cat. She wouldn't leave Joey behind. All the lights were off except one lamp by the door and the hallway light. Almost as if she was lighting a path to his bedroom. He grinned. She was waiting for him.

A wave of panic rolled over him, but he did his best to shrug it off. He was Gallant Lake's confirmed bachelor, but not in a playboy sort of way. More like when-was-the-last-time-anyone-saw-him-date sort of way. He was the geeky dude who collected old things and sold exciting stuff like bolt cutters and pliers. He and Maggie Hall had dated for a while six years ago, but had decided they were better friends than lovers. Things had been a bit more serious with Renee Cooper three years back. She was a competitive snowboarder—younger, daring and adventurous. She'd come to town that winter to get back in shape after an injury, and somehow had been interested in the hardware guy. But she'd never reached the same seriousness about their relationship as Nate had. They'd had fun, which was apparently all Renee had been looking for. When the following winter approached, she'd kissed him goodbye and gone back on the snowboarding circuit.

Nate shook his head sharply. Why was he doing this trip down memory lane *now*? There was a fascinating woman waiting for him In. His. Bed. Sure, he was a little out of practice, but it was like riding a bike, right? It wasn't like he'd forgotten his way around a woman. But this felt bigger than that. This was Brittany Doyle. And for all their one-night-stand talk, he had a hunch things could get a lot more complicated than that in a hurry. He grinned and turned off the lights on his way to his bedroom. She was worth the risk, and he was done questioning this.

She was lying on the bed, stretched out on her side, supporting her head on one arm. Her capris were gone, but she still wore his T-shirt. It was sexier than any piece of lacy lingerie. Her hair was pulled back in a messy knot, and he decided that wasn't going to do at all. He wanted that brown hair splayed out on the pillow for him. But he could take care of that…once he got into bed with her.

He shucked his jeans and shirt, kicking them into the corner of the room as he closed the door behind him and made sure it was latched tightly. No more doggy interruptions tonight. Brittany watched him in silence, with the corner of her mouth twitching. Nerves? Humor? Both? He walked toward the bed. Her mouth twitched some more, and she sucked on her bottom lip to stop it. He knelt on the side of the king-size bed, then started crawling toward her on his hands and knees. No more doubts. No more thoughts at all, other than pleasing this woman.

His first move was to reach up and free her hair, running his hands through it and spreading it out like tawny brown flames on the pillow.

"You having fun?" She arched her brow at him, but her voice was more purr than sass.

"Mmm-hmm." He traced his fingers down her cheek to cup her chin. "You keep that hair all buttoned up and confined, but I like it like this…wild and natural." He leaned in for a soft kiss on her mouth, and it was a struggle to pull away. But he didn't want to rush this. Just in case it *was* a one-night stand, he was determined to make every minute count.

"Two words rarely associated with me." A tiny wrinkle appeared between her brows. "Maybe because I'm always so buttoned up."

Nate kissed that little wrinkle until it was smooth once again. "I like seeing you unbuttoned. It's like having my own secret Brittany that no one else knows."

Her eyes darkened, making the gold flecks sharpen in contrast. She raised her head and kissed him hard and…wild. Her fingernails dug into his bare back, making him grunt, but he didn't want her to stop. He drove his tongue past hers, and she didn't concede right away. No surprise there. The fight was half the fun with her. His hands found the bottom of her/his shirt and started tugging it up. She arched her back to help and reached for his briefs, sliding them to his thighs and freeing his arousal.

All he wanted was to bury himself in her, but no. *Take your time.* But Brittany had another plan. As he moved to shed the briefs completely, she wrapped her hands around him and gripped and loosened in a rhythm that made him feel like his brain was melting.

"Ah…oh, damn…babe…" *Stop. Don't stop…*

He yanked hard on the T-shirt, temporarily tying up her hand as he pulled it off over her head. She was laughing again, but it wasn't a giddy laugh. It was a whiskey laugh, rough and deep and, like everything else she'd done tonight, sexy as all get-out. He looked down at her and blinked. She was naked now, and...perfect. Not bathing-suit-model perfect, but real-woman perfect. Perfect for *him*, and him alone. He'd said earlier she was his secret. *His.* Maybe not forever, but damn, for tonight it was true. She was his. And she was perfect.

He fell on her, holding her head in his hands and kissing her long and deep and hard. She was trying to reach him again, but he was already between her legs, rocking against her. She wasn't going to take over. Not tonight. Her moan was half lusty laughter and half frustration. Since she couldn't reach her target—no way he'd last if she touched him there again—she gripped his butt cheeks and pulled him almost into her.

"Slow down, kitten..." He rubbed against her, but slowly. Her eyes snapped open, and he saw an angry glint in them. He chuckled. "Not a criticism, babe. I just want a chance to explore you a little."

Her body relaxed, but she shook her head. "Explore later. I need you right now."

"What you *don't* need is a surprise nine months from now." He shifted, reaching for his nightstand and silently praying there were still a few condoms in there. There were, thank God. He held up a foil pack, and her eyes widened.

"There are advantages to a man who always

keeps his head…" Realizing what she'd just said, she laughed. "Oh, you know what I mean. Here, let me do that."

He handed it to her, but held her hand closed around it. Her rushing was hot, but worrisome.

"Brittany, you know I'm ready…" He rocked again, making her moan. "But I want more of you tonight than this." He squeezed her hand. "Don't get me wrong—I want *this*. And *now*. But I also want to taste you from your toes to your hair and everywhere in between. And I do mean *everywhere*." She smiled softly, her eyes shining. He got lost in those eyes for a moment, then regrouped. "We've hardly done anything, and already I know this is going to be…"

"Nate…honey…" She pinched his chin with her thumb and forefinger. "Stop talking. Stop fretting. Stop thinking. Just because I said I need you right now doesn't mean I'm going anywhere." She tipped his chin down and kissed the tip of his nose, making his arousal surge against her leg. She grinned. "It just means you've turned me into a horny mess and I'm seriously going to lose my mind if you don't do this thing. Hard and fast and good. Right now. After that, there are a few places on you that *I* want to explore. We've got all night for the slow and sultry stuff. But right now?" She lifted his chin, a playful, seductive gleam in her eye. "Right now I need you to get that condom on and do the deed, okay?"

Something hot and oddly comforting rose in his

chest as she told him what she needed. Trusting him to deliver. Promising more.

More...

He wanted that. Not the sex, although he sure as hell wanted that. But he wanted more of *her.* He was falling hard for this funny, feisty woman in his arms. He probably needed to think about that discovery, but not right now. She was right—the time for thinking was over.

He slipped on the condom and held himself up on his forearms, staring straight down at her as he moved against her and then away, teasing her until a tiny glistening tear appeared at the corner of her eye. He kissed that sucker away and slid into her in the same instant. They both let out matching sighs as he did. He stopped, eyes tightly closed, trying to maintain some modicum of control as he wrapped his mind around how good she felt. How perfect she felt. Like no other woman.

Like she was *his* woman.

Brittany's fingers tightened on Nate's shoulders and didn't let go. She wanted this moment to last forever. The heat, the tenderness, the rush of desire, the sensations that kept skipping across her skin. Neither of them moving, neither of them breathing... She wanted to linger here and revel in all of it. How could it get any better?

Then he started to slowly rock against her, easing in and out with such precision that she let out a long, low moan. She barely managed to avoid saying the words out loud—*don't stop*. Nate's lips brushed her ear.

"Oh, Britt…ah…you're freakin' perfect, babe. You're perfect…"

Her heart leaped. He thought she was *perfect*? No one had ever used that word to describe her, and certainly never during sex. Her hips rose to match his rhythm, and she stopped thinking entirely. He muttered something that sounded vaguely vulgar, and she just nodded against him. The sheets twisted around their legs as the pace picked up. A switch had been flipped for both of them, and it was *on*. Just what she'd begged for—fast, hard and intense.

"I'm ready…" She gasped.

"Go, babe. I've got you."

She cried out…something. *His* name? God's name? Maybe just a garble of sounds? She had no idea. She was too busy trying to recover from the free fall. Nate was right behind her and had the same problem with articulation. A grunt. A cry. And release. They clung to each other, both gasping to catch their breath, for a long silent moment.

He nuzzled her neck softly. "Um…wow."

She breathed out a low laugh. "Um…yeah."

Another nuzzle. A kiss. And he moved, sliding off to the side and disposing of the condom before quickly bringing her in for a tight embrace. His gaze moved over her face as if he was in awe. She was feeling the same way. His mouth slid into a wry grin.

"Well, that was fun."

"So much fun that I'm wondering if you just made up all that hemming and hawing and *out of practice* nonsense earlier."

Nate laughed. "Why do you say that?"

"For someone who kept whining 'I'm not a player!', you've got game, Nate Thomas. Serious game." He'd made her feel like she never had before—turned on and happy and safe all at the same time. She was still glowing from the sensation, hoping it never faded.

He kissed the back of her neck. "A woman like you makes a man want to up his game, Brittany Doyle. I'm glad you were satisfied."

Satisfied? She was so much more than that. But before she could say so, he fell silent, his body relaxing behind her. He was falling asleep. It was hardly a surprise, since the poor guy had only had a few hours' sleep in the past twenty-four hours and had worked hard all day. She stayed quiet, listening to the change in his breathing as he drifted into slumber. Something warm and funny happened in her chest. Her feelings for Nate were brand-new. More than just the sexual chemistry, there was something that felt like a true bond forming between them. A *strong* bond of caring and connecting and…something else. Something she wasn't ready to name yet. Instead, she closed her eyes, knowing she hadn't had much more sleep than he'd had.

A bright light woke her, and for a second she thought they'd slept the night away. She felt a stab of disappointment, since Nate had said he wanted to explore every inch of her that night. She held up her hand to cover her eyes and felt him shift behind her.

"I guess the power's back on." He stretched and sat up. "The generator only covers certain breakers and that wasn't one of them."

"Oh, good. I thought it was morning!"

Nate looked down at her, laughing. "And that would be tragic because…?"

Her cheeks warmed, but she figured she'd already seduced the man, so it was too late to be demure.

"Because you promised me a long night of slow, sizzly sex." She brushed her hair off her face. "And I'd hate to think we both slept through it."

Nate tipped his head back and laughed. He sounded so relaxed and grounded compared to her nerves, which were suddenly running all over the place. He leaned down and kissed her forehead.

"Well, good news, kitten. It's not even midnight. Are you hungry?"

She hadn't thought she was, but as soon as he asked, she realized she hadn't had anything since she and Nora ate some fast-food burgers that someone had delivered early in the afternoon.

"Actually, yes. I could eat, but not a lot."

"Stay right there." He stood, tugging on a pair of gym shorts that were hung on the back of a chair. "I'll make sure the generator's off and check the lights. Then I'll make us some sandwiches and grab a couple beers." He arched one brow. "Or wine?"

She stretched, feeling a few protests from parts of her body that hadn't been used in a while. But the pain was sweet and totally worth it. Damn, they'd had a good time earlier.

Nate chuckled. "If you don't stop looking at me with those do-me eyes, there won't be any food because I'll crawl right back into bed. Beer or wine?"

"Beer's fine." He headed to the door, but she stopped him as he reached for it. "And by the way, we can have both."

He looked over his shoulder, confused. She clarified with a wink.

"We can have food and *then* you can crawl back into bed with me."

And that was what they did. Nate made sandwiches with thinly sliced turkey and Swiss cheese on toasted kaiser rolls. And a plate of grapes. Brittany had pulled Nate's T-shirt back on and was perched on the bed when he brought them in. He joined her there, picnic style on the sheets. Brittany held her sandwich up and sniffed it, then laughed in surprise.

"Only a bachelor would put tartar sauce on turkey. Tartar's for *fish*, Nate."

He took a huge bite of his sandwich, unconcerned, then closed his eyes in appreciation.

"Have you tried it?" He was talking around his food, so she wasn't sure she'd heard him right.

"What?"

He swallowed. "Have you tried it?" He lifted his sandwich for another bite. "Before you get on your high horse, you might want to taste it first."

"I don't have a high horse." She sniffed. Then she met his gaze and her shoulders dropped. She couldn't fool this man. "Okay, maybe I have a *medium* horse. But not a high one."

They both laughed, and she took a bite of the sandwich. Her eyes went wide.

"Oh, damn. That's…good!" It was sharp and tart and it worked. "Who taught you that trick?"

"No one. Being a bachelor—" he winked "—sometimes means making do with what you have. One day all I had was tartar sauce for my sandwich. And it tasted good."

She nodded in agreement, leaning back against the headboard and stretching her legs in front of her. "So you've always been a confirmed bachelor?"

He didn't answer right away, chewing his sandwich and staring down at the sheets between them. "I don't know how *confirmed* I was, but that's how it worked out. It's not like I never ever dated, but it's a small town and…"

"And you ran out of prospects?"

Nate barked out a laugh. "Something like that. When you're friends with people, and they're friends with your friends, things get weird in a hurry if you change the dynamic. That's why I don't do…"

"One-night stands?" She fought the frown that started to pull at her. She'd talked him into this. And it definitely had changed the dynamic of their relationship. What if this was a huge mistake? As if he'd read her mind, Nate reached out and patted her leg.

"Hey, I wasn't saying anything about us, kitten. I'm talking about *me* being the hardware guy everyone in town knows. It's awkward if I start dating someone local. Everyone in town gets…invested." He finished the last of his sandwich.

"And you don't think they'll be invested in *us*?"

It was one of those moments when her thoughts occurred out loud as she thought them. She was just as surprised as Nate was, and they stared at each other. Were they dating? Or was this really just a one-night stand? The thought made her heart feel pinched and tight. Nate set his plate on the nightstand and moved closer to her, taking her hand.

"Okay, let's talk about that. Do you want an *us*? I mean…what are we doing here exactly?"

Of *course* she wanted an *us*. Maybe not long-term, but for now. Until he learned why she was in Gallant Lake. Until he learned she'd been lying about buying property. She blinked back a shocking rush of tears burning her eyes. That would end everything.

"Whoa." Nate moved quickly to take her in his arms, his fingers brushing her face. "What's this? Let's save this conversation for morning." He kissed her temple, holding his mouth against her skin. "I don't know how we got from tartar sauce to this, but forget it. We had plans for tonight, remember?" He pulled his head back and stared straight into her eyes. "And if we decide in the daylight tomorrow that we want to keep this going, then I won't give a damn what people get invested in. Like you said, we're adults here."

"Do you want to keep going after tonight?" She didn't understand why, but she needed to know.

The corner of his mouth twitched before he grew serious. "Yeah, I do. We both know one night isn't going to be enough. As long as we stay honest with each other, Britt, I don't see why not. How about you?"

There was the one word she couldn't swear to. *Honesty.* She'd already left two messages for Conrad this week, suggesting he reconsider his plans for Gallant Lake. She told him the town was going to fight the project. The problem was, she had three property owners who were ready to sell. But Conrad didn't know that yet. She swallowed hard, trying to figure out a way to answer.

"You're right, Nate. One night won't cut it with us. So we'll play it by ear. I hate to sound so cliché, but we can take it a day at a time, right?" She skipped right over that *honesty* thing.

Nate's smile deepened. "Even better, let's take it an hour at a time. A minute at a time. We don't need to go past that right now. We don't need to go past this minute right here, Britt." He kissed her softly, pulling her in even closer. Her hand caressed his bare chest as he kept talking, his voice low. "And right this minute I need to keep my promise. I'm going to explore you for the rest of the night, and right into the morning if we can." Another kiss. "And I'm gonna start…" A kiss. "Right now."

He cupped her face in his hands and kissed her deeply this time, making her forget everything but how he made her feel. His hands slid down her arms and they both slid down to the mattress. Her shirt came off. His briefs came off. And Nate Thomas fulfilled his promise. Slowly. Carefully. Seductively. Fingertips. Mouth. Body. He took her to the edge over and over again, leaving her pleading. Finally granting her the release she needed, then starting all over again. Her body was humming with a dizzying blend of satisfaction and desire.

No, one night would *never* be enough with this man. She couldn't help wondering if any number of nights would be enough. She had a feeling her body would never be satisfied with anyone else. Ever.

Chapter Eleven

Nate made pancakes.

It wasn't like he needed comfort food after all the...um...comfort he got last night with Brittany. But he was restless that morning, and pancakes—from scratch, not a box—required some attention. Concentrating helped settle him, and he needed that. Their night together had been amazing. This felt like a defining moment. Like everything in his life as he knew it had been forever altered. As if he might look at things as being before Brittany and after Brittany. And that was the part that created the tightness in his chest this morning. What was *after Brittany* going to look like?

"Something smells delicious." Her voice was

husky from lack of sleep as she slid her arms around him from behind. "And I am officially starving. Is there coffee in this establishment?"

And just like that, his worries were gone. Her touch did that to him. Calmed him. Steadied him. He nodded toward the coffee maker.

"Hot and ready. But you'll have to use milk for creamer. I drink it black, and I wasn't expecting overnight guests." He hadn't been expecting *any-thing* that happened in the past twenty-four hours.

She moved away, patting him on the back as she did. "I'll forgive you this time, but in the future, I prefer French vanilla creamer, thank you very much."

In the future.

That meant she wanted last night to happen again. Probably a big mistake. But one he was totally on board with making. The tops of the pancakes were bubbling, so he flipped them. A minute later he was sliding them onto a plate for her and pointing to the silverware drawer. It felt so…normal. Having a woman here in the morning. Making her breakfast. As if it happened all the time.

Which was almost laughable, because it hadn't happened in *years*. And the few times a woman had woken up at his place, he'd never made her pancakes. He'd usually just had a cup of coffee waiting, and his guests had gone on their way.

He looked to where Brittany sat at the 1950s enamel-topped kitchen table, wearing one of his flannel shirts like a robe over one of his T-shirts. Her long legs and bare feet were wrapped around the metal legs of the kitchen chairs. Her hair was pulled up on top of her head and secured somehow, but not well. It was loose and wild, with long strands breaking free and curling down around her neck. Without her usual designer armor on, she looked like she belonged there, stuffing her face enthusiastically with his pancakes.

He smelled something burning and quickly flipped the cakes he was making for himself. They were going to be a little crisp on that side, but that was okay. Right now *everything* felt okay.

"Mmm," Brittany moaned. "These may just be the best pancakes I've had in my life, Nate. So freakin' good!" She looked around the kitchen, with its bright yellow walls and black-and-white-checkerboard tile floor. "I feel like I've stepped back in time. But it's… cute."

His face twisted.

"*Cute* wasn't exactly what I was going for." He joined her at the table. "How about…authentic? Period appropriate? Attractive?"

Her eyes shone with laughter and something hotter, too. "I think *authentic* works. And *attractive*." She winked, and he knew she wasn't talking about the kitchen anymore. "As for *period appropriate*, I'm not sure about that. You're a man for *all* periods. Except maybe the current one."

He chewed his pancake and thought about that for a moment, then grinned.

"I disagree. You're the epitome of current times, and I think I did just fine with you last night."

She laughed, pulled one foot up onto the chair seat and hugged her knee as she sipped her coffee. "You did more than fine last night. That was fun. Really fun." She hesitated, her laughter fading. "It was special, Nate."

"It was."

She set her coffee down and stared at him.

"So now what?"

"That's the hundred-thousand-dollar question, isn't it?" He blew out a breath. "Didn't we decide we'd take it a day at a time?"

That felt too temporary for Nate's liking. Too fragile. She seemed to feel the same way.

"I know I said I'm fine with the occasional, consensual one-night stand. But we have something…" Her shoulder lifted, then fell. "It feels like something that should be explored, doesn't it?"

Before he could answer, Joey came trotting into the kitchen, sniffing the air, his tail wagging. Brittany laughed.

"Well, good morning, Joe! Did you smell breakfast?" She reached down and scratched the dog's ears. Her voice was practically cooing. "That's usually what it takes to get you up in the morning, isn't it, you lazybones?" She stood and gave Joey a piece of pancake before putting her dish in the sink. "We have a routine. I need to let him out. Then he gets breakfast. Then he sleeps again until our noontime walk." She opened the door for Joe.

"For someone who insisted she wasn't keeping that dog, it sounds like you've become a permanent matched set."

She walked to the back door. "He's a great companion, but nothing in my life is permanent." The words had been tossed over her shoulder casually, but that was not how they landed. She caught up with the change in the room's atmosphere a moment after he did. "Nate...I didn't mean to sound so coldhearted about it. But let's face it. Whether it's a dog or a guy, nothing stays in my life for long."

"Why do you think that is?"

Her forehead furrowed in thought.

"I'm just not wired that way, I guess. It's not in my nature to get attached."

"Because of how you grew up?"

Her eyes went steely. "What do *you* know about how I grew up?"

"Nothing!" He raised his hands. "You mentioned not having a lot as a kid, and I thought that might be why you don't get attached." He walked to the sink with his empty plate, then turned to pull her into his arms. "You know how curious I can be, but I didn't mean to grill you. If you don't want to talk about it, then don't."

She rested her head on his shoulder with a heavy sigh. They stood like that, just holding each other silently. After a few moments he could feel the tension leaving her. He kissed the top of her head, but waited for her to speak first.

"Okay, here's the deal." She took a breath, then rushed ahead. "I never knew my dad. He left my mom when I was a baby, probably because Mom was a barely functioning alcoholic. She couldn't hang on to a job. She couldn't hang on to an apartment. She met some other random guy and had my little sister, and the dad took off." She tipped her head back, looking at him with a sad smile. "Do you sense a pattern there, Dr. Freud?" She rested her forehead on his chest as if she couldn't tell the story while looking into his eyes. "There were a lot of nights when our bed was the back seat of her old Toyota."

His heart felt like it was in a vise.

"You were homeless?"

She nodded against him. "We managed to stay a step above the cardboard box and shopping cart kind of homeless, but not by much. The car at least gave us a roof and locking doors. And it was always temporary. A few nights while she tried to find a new place. A few weeks if things got really bad."

"I'm so sorry, babe."

She stayed in his arms a bit longer, then pulled back. She raised her chin and straightened her shoulders. She was pulling up her defenses. Even her voice got an edge to it.

"Don't be sorry for me. We made it. At least, Ellie and I did. She graduates college next spring. And I've made sure neither one of us will ever go through that again."

If his heart had been squeezed before, it felt shattered now. There was so much to unpack in those sentences. Especially that last one. *I've made sure...* Brittany had single-handedly taken it on her shoulders to protect her sister and herself. That explained a lot. Why she was so driven. Why she wore her expensive clothes. Why she held everyone at an arm's length.

"And your mom?"

She blinked and looked away, her voice hard, but cracking just a little. She wasn't as tough as she let on.

"She died when I was in college. She got in with a worse crowd than usual and started using drugs. Just like everything else, she was really bad at it. She OD'd." She took a breath, trying to smile again. "I worked two jobs to keep a roof over Ellie's and my heads. She's diabetic, and once she started on insulin, I dropped school and just worked nonstop to cover the bills. I finished my degree online a few years later. And here I am, in Gallant Lake. Sleepin' with a picker."

He chuckled. She was changing the subject, and he was glad to follow along.

"You're lowering your standards, Britt."

"On the contrary." Her smile softened, becoming more genuine. "At the risk of inflating your ego, you raised the standards, Nate. Which brings us back to the original question. What now?"

The dog yipped outside the door, so Nate let him inside and put some food down before turning back to Brittany.

"I agree with what you said before. This feels… special. What we have. How you make me feel. I don't want to lose it. If it doesn't freak you out too much, let's see where it takes us."

"You know I can't…"

"Stay? Yeah, I know." He didn't like thinking about it, but he understood it a whole lot more after what she'd just shared. "But until that time comes, let's explore what we have."

She stepped into his open arms and kissed him. "Do you mean right now literally? Like…let's go do some exploring? Right…" She kissed him again. "Now?" Another kiss.

"Let me call Darius and make sure he can open the store for me." He kissed her again, hating what he had to say next. "But I'm going to have to go in eventually. After the storm, people are going to need supplies, and it'll get busy."

She smiled against his lips. "So what are we waiting for?"

What indeed? He followed her into his bedroom, making sure to latch the door so they wouldn't be interrupted. He wanted to give her his full attention. It might have to be fast, but that didn't mean he couldn't be thorough.

Brittany stretched and yawned, feeling both exhausted and invigorated. And maybe a little sore in a few spots. She looked around Nate's bedroom. She barely remembered him saying goodbye.

He was needed at the hardware store. The town was relying on him. She stretched again, then sat up, hugging her knees. She was falling for a guy people relied on. Was he someone *she* could rely on? Joey scratching at the bedroom door was what finally got her out of bed, although the movement made her groan. She checked the bedside clock, stopped, then checked it again. How could it be almost one o'clock? She had to get dressed and get home. But… wearing what? Her clothes from yesterday were dirty and sweaty. She had no desire to put them back on today. That was when she saw that Nate had, once again, thought ahead.

A pair of sweats—presumably his—were folded on a carved oak dining chair by the door, with a T-shirt—definitely one of his—on top of it. And a note sat on the shirt.

I tossed your stuff in the washer. Figured this was enough while you wait. Back in a while—pasta okay for dinner? Text if not. Nate.

She couldn't help but smile as she reached for her phone to text him.

Pretty cocky to assume I'm staying for dinner.

It was only a minute before a reply came back.

Are you just getting up, lazybones?

She watched as the little bubbles swam on the screen before another text came through.

BTW, I'm hoping you stay for more than dinner.

She pulled on the sweats and shirt and let a whining Joey outside before answering. It took her that long to decide what she was willing to commit to.

Let's start with dinner. Which I will make. I'm afraid you'd use ketchup for sauce.

Nate sent an LOL emoji, followed with his answer.

Coward! But okay. Busy here, but I'll be home by 6:30.

She checked to make sure Joey was staying close by. As usual, his goal seemed to be to sniff every inch of the yard, which would take him a while. Nate's front yard wasn't that large, but his backyard widened and ran to the lakeshore. He'd lost one fair-size tree in the storm, but it was already cut into sections and stacked by the remains of the stump, thanks to all the helpers yesterday. But the largest oaks and maples had survived and were shading the yard from the bright sun, creating dappled patterns of light and dark across the grass. It made a pretty picture, especially with the bright blue water of Gallant Lake as a backdrop. Two intricate iron benches sat near the water, painted green and looking as if they'd been there forever. But she recognized them from the barn sale on the Day of the Kiss. She'd commented to Nate that they were pretty, and now there they sat, on his waterfront. She smiled, feeling a warm sensation near her heart. Had he bought them with the thought that she'd be here someday? Or had they simply reminded him of her?

She found his laundry room and put her wet clothes into the dryer. It gave her pause when she held her underwear in her hand. Which meant they'd been in Nate's hand. There was a quick blush of embarrassment until she realized he'd had every inch of body in his hands last night, so her underwear wasn't such a big deal. Joey yipped at the door to come in. As he curled up on the sofa three feet from Nate's cat, Brittany took an inventory of his kitchen. She jotted a shopping list of what she'd need—everything—and waited for her clothes to dry.

While she waited, she checked out the house. She'd been there two nights now, but the first night she was too exhausted from the storm to notice many details, and last night she'd been too…um…*busy* to notice. The place was thoroughly Nate from wall to wall. Chock-full of antiques and collectibles. Some were hanging on the wall in interesting and colorful little groupings. Most of the seating, like the sofa where she'd woken up in Nate's arms the night before, seemed newer and designed for comfort. Nothing fancy, to be sure, but practical. The tables and hutches, however, were clearly antiques from various eras. From the simple lines of a few arts-and-crafts small tables and a plain shaker corner cupboard to a couple of ornately carved Victorian items, it all just worked. His home was charming and eclectic, bordering on eccentric—but not quite. A lot like Nate.

Once her clothes were dry, she changed and headed to the grocery store, then stopped at the liquor store to grab some wine. Mack was there, restocking shelves. She greeted Brittany with a smile, explaining that the post-storm rush on alcohol had been good for business.

"Clearly, everyone wiped out their liquor cabinets during the blackout." She laughed as she added three bottles of wine to a display. "Including you, I guess."

Brittany shook her head absently, holding a bottle

of sauvignon so she could read the label. "I'm cooking, and Nate's house has more beer than wine, so…" She stopped as soon as she realized what she'd just disclosed. Mack was staring at her with a wide smile and a curious gleam in her eye.

"You're cooking at *Nate's* house? How cozy. And intimate. And…" She gestured at Brittany. "Come on. Help me fill in the blanks, girl. Is this a friendly neighbor sort of dinner, or a let's-eat-before-hopping-into-bed sort of thing?"

She chewed her lip before answering. "Probably closer to the last one."

Mack's eyebrows shot up under her thick blond hair.

"You sound awfully casual about that. Which tells me it won't be the first time you've hopped in bed together. Damn, Brittany. Sit down and tell me what I've missed!"

"I can't. I have groceries in the car, including chicken breasts. I need to run… Bye!" She turned to bolt, but Mack stopped her, handing her a bottle of white wine.

"First, use this unoaked chardonnay for cooking— it's dry, crisp and cheap. And take this pinot grigio to serve with the meal. It's very nice and…" She winked. "Nate told me he liked it when he came to a tasting here a few months ago."

"I'm trying to picture Nate at a wine tasting." She thought of his beer stash in the refrigerator.

Mack nodded. "I get that. But can you picture him helping out a fellow business owner? No one cares more about the success of the downtown businesses than Nate Thomas. It was his idea to have a wine tasting specifically for guys who did't drink wine. We had a great turnout, too."

Brittany could totally see that happening. Nate cared so much about this little town. And he was going to care a *lot* about it being forever altered by Conrad's condos. She paid for the wine and went home, making a quick stop at the cottage for another change of clothes—just in case—and her laptop. She checked her emails while sitting on the back deck at Nate's place, with a tall glass of lemonade on the table next to her. It was a near-perfect day—warm and bright, with puffy white clouds drifting across a sharp blue sky that cast round shadows on the side of Gallant Mountain. She could get used to working here, in the comfort of a giant old Adirondack chair at Nate's house with this view.

But her first email sent a shadow over the afternoon. It was from Conrad:

You seem concerned about community reception to our plans. That's something you've never worried about before, but fine. Of course you can't share these, but here are the artist renderings of what we'll be building in Gallant Lake. It should make you feel better. It's not some monstrosity. It's clean, modern and, best of all, profitable. Don't let me down, Barracuda. I'm counting on you for this one.

To be fair, Conrad had built some very nice communities and resorts in the past. Sometimes change was good, and maybe she needed to have a more open mind about her employer's plans. She clicked on the attachment. And gasped so loudly that Joey looked up from his resting spot next to her.

The drawing showed a long cement-and-cedar building, three stories high, along Main Street. Everything was horizontal on it, from the layout of the cedar planks on the second story to the windows, which were long and narrow toward the street. It looked like a prison, or maybe like a city office building that had been pancaked and plopped into Gallant Lake. On the water side, the second story was a wall of floor-to-ceiling windows. That made sense with the view, but the interior sketches screamed "city loft" far more than "Catskills charm."

The ground floor had some retail shops, but many of the condos took the whole three stories. From the water it looked like one really long restaurant with that wide swath of windows. And from the street… the view Nora's customers would have…it was sterile. And ugly. And *nothing* like any of the existing buildings in town. She scrolled through the images again, then slammed her laptop shut, tears pushing at the corners of her eyes.

She'd done this job for years. She'd played a big role in changing the landscape of neighborhoods and towns. She'd always thought it was a good thing. She was helping to inject money and business into the local economies. Even the people who objected often ended up supporting Conrad's projects, because the guy was good at seeing potential growth. And growth helped everyone. Growth raised property values. Growth raised incomes as businesses catered to the new residents or tourists.

But it had never felt like this. It had never felt personal. As if it was *her* community being "improved" by Conrad Quest. *Her* friends staring at the garish new building. *Her* lover losing the character of the town his family had been part of for generations. She smiled. *Five* generations, to be exact. Nate liked to make that point often. She reached down to scratch Joey's head, sending his long hair flopping back and forth. It was time to make dinner. And while she did that, she'd start brainstorming ways to stop Conrad. Preferably without losing her job.

Ten days later she was still brainstorming. While Nate was at the store most days, she'd be online, researching other potential locations and crunching numbers. Because the only thing that mattered to Conrad was numbers. And she knew how to talk his language. She was going to save this damn town, one way or the other. Because she was falling for Nate Thomas, and falling hard.

The first few nights they'd alternated between his house and the cottage for sleeping and dinner. But as much as Brittany valued maintaining her independence, she was the first to point out it didn't make sense. Nate's house was spacious and had all the amenities. The cottage was…*not* spacious. And needed a lot of improvising to accommodate two people, with its limited kitchen space and tiny single bathroom. It also didn't have the big deck and comfy Adirondack chairs she liked so much. After four nights she'd packed up and basically moved in, using the cottage for work during the day, but that was it.

They continued to tell each other it was only temporary. *Someday* she'd have to go back to Tampa if she wanted to keep collecting paychecks and move into that partner's office. But she wasn't thinking about that now. She refused to think about it. Which might not be practical, but this feeling in her heart was so brand-new that she wanted to give it her full attention.

She and Nate made no sense on paper. She was driven. He was laid-back. She craved change—or at least she used to—and he valued the past above all else. He thought tartar sauce was a sandwich spread. She'd taken cooking classes at a four-star restaurant last fall. The contrasts went on and on. And while some people thought opposites-attract romances were a thing, the trope was unrealistic in movies and in books. And real life. Sure, things might be interesting and fun at first, but then someone always had to compromise, and how could that lead to any long-term happiness? Someone was always a winner, making the other a loser, right?

She started whipping the eggs with more force than necessary, considering they were just being used as a quick dip for the fish fillets Nate had pulled from the freezer the night before. He'd told her proudly that he'd caught and cleaned them himself, and he had assured her that freshwater perch were mild and tender when cooked right. Which she had taken as a challenge.

Joey and Pepper were sleeping on the sofa together, and no longer at opposite ends. They'd settled whatever cat vs. dog standoff they'd had in the beginning and were now fast friends. And sleeping buddies. Right now Joey was stretched out on the sofa, with Pepper curled up under his chin. They'd worked it out, and there didn't seem to be a winner or loser between them.

She warmed up the oil in the cast-iron skillet, knowing Nate would be home shortly. Their routine was comfortable. Natural. Just last night they'd been huddled together under a blanket on one of the Adirondack chairs, watching the moon rise over the lake and sipping hot cocoa. Nate had brushed his lips across her ear and whispered that it felt as if they'd been together "forever." That was a word she generally didn't believe in, but being with Nate was making her wonder.

Ellie had always insisted that there was a *someone* out there who'd make Brittany believe in forever someday. She'd always laughed at her little sister's rosy outlook, but maybe…just maybe…a guy like Nate could change her mind. His quiet strength settled her in ways she'd never experienced. And in bed… Well, in bed he made her feel things. Sexy things. Woman things. Most of all, he made her feel safe. From everything and everyone.

As a fiercely independent businesswoman, she'd never wanted or needed some man to protect her. She could take care of herself and had done so her entire adult life. But the security Nate gave her didn't take away from that. Unlike so many of the men she'd dated, Nate didn't need her to be less in order for him to be more.

Which meant the whole opposites-attract idea could work for them. But only as long as Nate never learned of her role with Conrad's plans. Nate might not need her to be less, but he did need her to be honest, and she hadn't been that. Not completely. She had a feeling honesty was the one thing he would never compromise on. Which would definitely make her the loser.

Chapter Twelve

Nate's life had been transformed. Oh, he still worked the store and worried about bills and went picking on the weekends. Same old life. But there was a bright new presence in it, in the shape of Brittany Doyle, shining light into every corner of his days and nights.

He'd always known there was chemistry there. The kiss in the barn a month ago made that very clear. He knew making love to her would change things. He just never knew how much. How much he'd crave her touch. And not just when they were together. His need for her was constant, like a gas burner turned on low at the back of the stove, keeping things warm until he was with her again.

Which was every night now. She'd moved into

his place by the end of the first week, declaring it was more "practical." He'd let her tell herself that, knowing she needed to cling to her independence. But Brittany staying at his house had nothing to do with practicality, unless it was the practicality of being able to get naked together at a moment's notice. Which they'd been doing a lot. He had a hunch she was falling just as hard as he was. She might not want to, but she was falling nonetheless. The hard-edged city girl was beginning to appreciate life in the Catskills.

Last week she'd fried up some perch fillets from the freezer, just like a good fisherman's woman would do. They were a little fancier than he'd have done, but they were also twice as good. Which was a theme in their lives these days. She made everything better. Walks on the lakeshore became opportunities to hold hands and laugh together. To teach her how to skip stones on the water. To see the changing fall colors of the trees through her eyes. To go antiquing together and tug her into a dusty corner in some shop or barn for a quick, hard kiss.

"She's a natural at this." Asher Peyton clapped Nate on the back. They were on the wide wraparound porch outside Asher and Nora's log home on the mountainside. Nora and Brittany were playing a modified game of soccer with Nora and Asher's grandson, Charlie, in the yard below, being careful to avoid the drop-off that provided stunning views of the lake and the mountains beyond it. It was hard to look at the sunset right now, with the sun hovering near the horizon like a brilliant red ball. Brittany slipped in the grass and went down on her behind with a surprised squeal. Nate tensed for a fraction of a second until he saw her jump back to her feet, chasing the three-year-old with a laughing threat of revenge.

"Oh, man, you've got it bad, don't you?" Asher chuckled at his side.

Nate blinked. "What do you mean?"

"I mean...you and Brittany are gettin' serious in a hurry. Those puppy-dog eyes of yours tell me you're a goner." Asher raised his glass of bourbon with a grin. "She's it for you, isn't she?"

He looked back to the two women and the little boy. Brittany was trying to protect her makeshift goal made of two sticks while Nora and the little boy pressed forward. Her arms were spread wide, her face lit up with laughter. When Charlie kicked the ball, she made a show of leaping for it, but he could tell she missed it on purpose, lying on the ground in defeat as it rolled between the sticks. Nora helped her up and they started back toward the house. Brittany looked up and caught his gaze, her smile deepening.

"Yeah," he said quietly. "She's it for me. But she's not staying..."

"Are you sure about that? Like I said, she looks like a natural. As if small-town living is where she belongs." Asher gave him a long look. "Or is it just because you're here? Did you ever consider she might think *you're* it for her, too? Have you guys not talked about this?"

"Like you said, it's happened fast. She's still got a job waiting in Tampa."

"She doesn't seem real eager to get back to that job."

It was true. She hadn't even mentioned it lately. But she had gone to the cottage, which she now referred to as her office, almost every day. She said she was handling emails and advising clients, but quickly changed the subject if he dug any deeper. She came onto the porch before he could respond to Asher, hooking her arm in his and giving him a quick kiss on the cheek. They walked inside, where Nora's stuffed shells were ready to come out of the oven. Brittany uncovered the salad she'd brought and added dressing, and they sat down to the meal as friends. They told stories and kept little Charlie entertained. The women sat at the kitchen island with their wine and giggled at the men's attempts to clean up after dinner. It was relaxing. It was fun. It felt like a peek through a door at the life Nate could have if she stayed. For all his protesting about change, the changes Brittany could bring to his life felt nothing but positive. And still he couldn't shake the feeling that there was something…some threat…hanging over their future together.

The next day he and Brittany returned the hosting favor, having a hamburger and sausage cookout before taking Asher and Nora out on Nate's antique boat, the *Gallant Lady*. The wooden Chris-Craft Continental was his pride and joy. His grandfather had bought the twenty-two-foot boat new in 1955. Nate had meticulously restored it over the years. It still had what collectors called an "original bottom," but the inboard engine, housed beneath a large wooden box in the center of the boat, was new. It had plenty of room to move around, with a bench seat across the back and a split bench at the helm. It was one of the few older things that Brittany had never once teased him about. She fell in love with it the first time he'd lowered it from the boathouse into the water.

She'd pronounced the boat an elegant and sexy classic, with long, sleek lines and the highly polished mahogany and teak. She also liked the raw power the boat had, and the smooth ride when the lake was choppy. She'd taken to the boating life and was driving it now, with Nora at her side. Nate and Asher sat in the back, enjoying a sip of whiskey from plastic cups. Brittany was new to driving, but they were out in deeper water, and the lake was surprisingly quiet for a Sunday afternoon, so there wasn't much to worry about. As if knowing this wasn't a time to be a hot-rodder, she was keeping a sedate cruising speed while she and Nora talked up front.

Asher nudged Nate's arm, gesturing to the two

women. "They're thick as thieves these days. I know I said this yesterday, but I want to be clear—if she's it for you, don't blow it. Ask her to stay, man. Look how happy she is. You guys have a good thing."

Brittany laughed as her hair started pulling free from the knot she'd tied it in. The wind whipped it around her shoulders and face, and she finally gave up, pulling all of it loose. She glanced back at him, and her face was lit with joy. It radiated from her like sunshine, and he knew his expression was probably the same. Brittany was one change he didn't want to avoid.

They were tidying up the kitchen later that night when he grabbed her by the waist and pulled her in for a kiss.

"Unhand me, sir!" She swatted his shoulder with a dish towel. "No distracting the…*help*!" The last word was shouted as he swung her around and pressed her against the old metal kitchen hutch. It rattled a bit but held firm when he lifted her up to sit there. At just the right height. Her eyes went dark and her smile moved from humor to heat. "What *are* you doing?"

Nate cupped her face with his hands.

"Loving you."

There. He'd said it. Her eyes went round, but he kissed away whatever she had to say. Getting the words out there was hard enough. He didn't want to analyze it right now. He just wanted to feel it. Revel in it. Make love to her with those words floating in the air above them. In that all-knowing way she had, Brittany read the need in his eyes like a book. She opened her legs so he could step inside them, pressing against her and kissing her with more raw desire than he'd ever felt before. She was his. *His*.

He felt that door to a future together open a little bit wider.

Asher was right. She was *it* for him.

She was everything.

"Conrad, I'm telling you Gallant Lake is a bad idea." Brittany tried to keep her voice level. If she couldn't deflect Conrad to something new and shiny, she was going to have to tell Nate, and everyone else, the truth about her role. "I sent you the information on that town in Connecticut, not far from the casino there, that got missed with the initial development that popped up. It's the same distance from Manhattan as Gallant Lake, and it's much more fiscally depressed, so people will be more eager to sell." Joey was lying on the sofa, tipping his head back and forth at her in curiosity, as he always did when she was on the phone.

"Brittany, if you can't handle this job," Conrad replied coolly, "tell me now so I can send someone else. My nephew keeps telling me he wants to prove himself."

There was a time not too long ago when those would have been fighting words. Brittany and Conrad's nephew, Kent, had been in competition for years. It was a battle largely manipulated by Conrad. He'd regularly pitted them against each other and then reaped the rewards when they went into overdrive to be the fastest and the best. Those days were over for her. She no longer felt the crushing need to prove herself to Conrad. His approval had always hinged on money. It had always been empty.

Over the past month or two, her drive to make more and more money had faded. Maybe Ellie had finally gotten through to her. Or maybe it was Nate, with his appreciation for repurposing old things and putting so much value on function. The way he appreciated what he had and where he was.

Money was never going to keep her warm at night the way Nate did. Would never give her the heart-deep joy of sitting on the dock in the morning with a hot mug of coffee and the man she loved. But as much as she wanted to tell her boss to go to hell, she couldn't afford to have Kent coming in to buy up the properties she was trying so hard to protect.

"There's no need to send Kent. I've *got* this." She put on her best barracuda voice, tough and confident. "I'm just looking out for the company's bottom line. With the resort already here and growing, people know what their properties could be worth. There's an active preservation society…" Run by Nate. "…that is not afraid to take developers to court. They did it with Blake Randall a few years back and *won…*"

Conrad talked right over her, suddenly angry. "I am *not* Blake Randall. Just because he *thinks* he's the kingpin of resort development doesn't mean it's true. He was born with a damn silver spoon in his mouth." He was almost yelling now, and she held the phone away and stared at it in confusion. Where was this coming from? "I can outwit that jackass with my eyes closed, Doyle, and don't you forget it. He may have caved to them, but I'm not afraid of a few local yokels."

"Don't call them that!" She clapped her hand over her mouth. It was a bad idea to elevate this. Especially when she had no idea why her boss was so irrationally angry. Conrad paused.

"Ex*cuse* me?"

"I mean..." She sighed. "Look, these people are smart and passionate about their town. You pay me to get the job done, but you also pay me for my experience and my ability to assess a situation in order to protect the bottom line. Right?"

He took a little longer to respond than she would have liked. Was he losing his faith in her? She couldn't afford to have that happen until she'd solved this mess. Instead of exploding, his voice settled a bit.

"That's right." Another pause. "But Gallant Lake is important to me. We need to make this work. I know you can do this for me. And there's a partnership waiting for you if you do."

That wasn't the enticement it had once been, but she didn't say so. Although she was curious.

"Why is this place so important, Conrad? Why are we doing this project differently from our usual, and very successful, approach?"

"Let's just say this one is personal. Make it happen."

She sat on the sofa after the call and scratched Joey's head, wondering what she was missing. Conrad said it was *personal*. He was one of the most ruthless businessmen she'd ever met. He hated any hint of people getting their emotions involved in their work. And what seemed to make it personal to him was Blake Randall. She knew about Randall Resorts International, but she'd never heard Blake's name mentioned before arriving in Gallant Lake, and never by Conrad until today.

She reached for her laptop. She was determined to get Conrad's sights off this town. It was time to research why his sights fell on it in the first place.

Chapter Thirteen

Nate tightened the tie-down straps holding the tall, heavily carved headboard to the side of the van. Brittany's eyes had lit up when she saw it the first time at the Kennedy place. Right before she smacked into that spider's web. Right before he kissed her. Right before he started to fall in love with her. At the time he'd dismissed the headboard as being too narrow. That was the problem with antique beds—they tended to be full-size or even smaller. Most clients wanted a minimum of queen-size.

Asher Peyton walked around the back of the van, carrying the footboard. He slid it into the van, and Nate wrapped a couple of blankets around it and strapped it to the opposite side. They lifted the side rails in last.

"Blanche told me her great-great-grandfather carved this bed from walnut trees he cut down on the farm over a hundred years ago." Nate gave the rails a pat. "Even after sitting in that abandoned house with no heat, it hasn't warped or split. That old man knew how to build." He looked at Asher. "You still think you can build this out to be a queen-size bed?"

"I'm a furniture maker by trade, Nate. Yes, I'm sure." Asher threw a blanket over the rails to keep them from sliding around. "Like I told you, I'll preserve the main sections of the headboard and footboard, but I'll have to add a lot of wood and match it the best I can. It means stripping and changing the structure of the original piece permanently, which isn't usually your thing." Asher looked up at him. "In fact, nothing about this is your thing. That bed's a little ornate for your place, and the dressing table is a bit…feminine."

He wasn't wrong. But it was the first antique Brittany had fallen for, and that made it special. If he could get her to stay, it might be *their* bed to be handed down over more generations. He just had to get her to stay. She was close; he was sure of that. They'd spent nearly every waking minute together since the storm, and the way she looked at him warmed him in a way no other woman had. She made him laugh, but even more important, he made *her* laugh. Every time she did, he could see more stress leave her shoulders. He could see more of the real Brittany.

He and Asher took the bedroom suite back to Asher's shop and unloaded it. This type of alteration wasn't something Asher normally did. He liked to build his own designs from scratch, not reconfigure someone else's work. But he and Nate had been friends for a long time, and he hadn't hesitated when Nate asked. They pushed the pieces together and tossed a canvas drop cloth over them.

"I can't keep them hidden all the time," Asher said, "but I'll do my best to keep my wife or her cousins from seeing an antique in my shop. They'd be asking questions nonstop, nosy biddies that they are." He winked, then grew more serious. "But I'm not gonna lie to my wife. If Nora asks, I'll have to tell her the truth. That's how love works." He paused. "Speaking of love, this bed wouldn't have anything to do with a pretty visitor to town, would it?"

He was usually pretty good at keeping a poker face when actually playing poker, but he couldn't stop the smile that formed. Talking about Brittany did that to him.

"It might." He tugged at the covering over the set. "She saw it a while back and liked it."

"She liked it." Asher opened the bottle of whiskey that sat on his workbench and grabbed two plastic cups, splashing a small amount of the amber liquid into them. "She just *liked* it and you're getting ready to spend a good amount of money making it work for her. A *bed*. That's quite a gift. Pretty intimate, if you ask me."

"Which I didn't, by the way." Nate accepted the glass of whiskey. "But if you must know, I'm trying to get her to hang around for a while. To give us a chance. And I'm not too proud to offer a bed as bribery."

"Ballsy. Nice." Asher drained his glass in one move. "So you think she might stay, huh? What about her job?"

Employment was the one area between them that had remained shrouded in foggy mystery. She said she was a consultant but had been perpetually vague when he'd pressed for any details. She'd change the subject and say it was boring or something like that. But he couldn't imagine Brittany doing anything boring. She was too driven. Competitive.

Asher sighed in satisfaction after finishing his drink.

"Did that friend of hers ever decide on a property to buy? Stella was complaining that her accepted offer has been sitting out there for a few weeks now."

Nate straightened. "Stella had an actual offer?"

"That's what she said. Brittany negotiated a price and took it to her buyer."

"But…Louise DiAngelo told me *she'd* agreed on

a price." He frowned. "Why would anyone want two storefronts that aren't connected?"

Why hadn't Brittany mentioned either deal to Nate?

Asher put his hands on his lower back and stretched. "I don't know, man. Ask your girl. Damn, I must be getting old. My back is screaming. If you don't mind, I think I'll head home to my wife and talk her into spending some time in the whirlpool with me."

Nate couldn't get the question out of his mind, even after heading back to his shop. He and Brittany had bared their souls—and their bodies—to each other. But he'd always felt she was holding something back.

Hank called out as soon as Nate walked into the shop. "Come spend your money! Come spend your money!"

That was a gem that Darius had taught him. Nate had been annoyed at first, but it turned out customers loved it and always laughed.

He tossed the bird a banana chip. "I spend enough money on you, you old fleabag."

Hank scrambled to the top corner of the cage, hanging sideways with one foot while chomping at the chip.

Darius came from the back storeroom. "Oh, hi, Nate. S'been a decent day so far. Old man Clifton cleaned us out of copper hinges for some remodeling project, and the resort sent someone in to order five dozen shelf supports for the new maintenance shed they're building, and they bought a bunch of line for their boat dock, too." The kid stopped for a second, screwing his face up, then snapping his fingers. "Oh, and Mrs. DiAngelo was looking for you. She has a question and apparently didn't trust me with it." He shrugged, unoffended. "But she was headed to Albany for something today, so she said it could wait until Monday. Oh, and listen to this… Hank, are you bringing sexy back?"

Hank let out a whistle, then started bobbing his head.

"Bringing sexy back! Bringing sexy back!"

Great.

"I know you love teaching him new stuff, but let's keep the sex talk to a minimum, Darius." His scolding lost its effect as Hank kept repeating the phrase, until Nate finally laughed at his bird. "Not cool, Hank."

"Bringing sexy back!"

Nate narrowed his eyes at Darius, who just shrugged again. The kid never seemed to get ruffled.

"It's not *my* fault your bird mimics everything. Say something often enough around him and he'll figure out how to repeat it. And how bad can that song be? My grandma uses it as her ringtone!"

Nate checked the levels in Hank's water bottles. "Maybe don't say stuff over and over again and he'll stop doing that." He waved Darius toward the back corner. "And your grandma is too frisky for her age, kid. Before you head out, we need to move some of that summer seeding and stuff to make space for snow shovels and ice melter. I've got an order coming in at the end of the month."

The days were getting shorter and the air was more crisp. Seasons were changing in the Catskills. As he and Darius shifted merchandise around, Nate couldn't help but wonder if Brittany would still be here when the first snowflakes flew. He *thought* she was falling as hard as he was, but she was still holding something back.

After the way she grew up, it was understandable. She'd been the family protector since she was a kid, and her fallback position was caution and skepticism. He'd have to be patient and try not to take it personally. He just needed to work harder to gain her complete trust.

Brittany was surprised to see Nate sitting on the steps to her cabin when she got back from visiting Blake and Amanda Randall at Halcyon. She'd reached out to Cassie Zetticci at the resort to ask a few discreet questions, but Cassie must have mentioned the conversation to her boss, Blake. She should have known she couldn't do anything under the radar in a small town. But in this case, she was happy Cassie had squealed on her.

It was Amanda who'd called, inviting her up to the big stone house for coffee and a slice of fresh-baked apple pie. They'd barely sat down when Blake joined them in the sunny solarium. Charming as always, it still didn't take him long to turn to her and pointedly ask who her mystery buyer *really* was and what she was doing here. She hadn't wanted to have that conversation with anyone in town before she'd talked to Nate, but she was also dying to know what the story was between Blake and Conrad. Her career at Quest Properties was over anyway, so she told him. After he'd finished laughing, Blake told her the whole story. And suggested a secret partnership of his own to replace the one she was about to lose with Conrad.

Feeling energized now that she hopefully had a way to get herself out of this mess, she gave Nate a bright smile. He stood and headed her way, returning her smile.

God, she hated lying to this man. She'd just been sworn to secrecy…again. But Blake assured her it was only temporary, and if all went well, she'd be able to give Nate—and Gallant Lake—the best news ever. Such good news that he'd *have* to forgive her for not being honest from the start. She hoped. Her chin lifted. She was The Barracuda. She could sell ice to polar bears. She could definitely make Nate see how much she loved him, and then he'd *have* to forgive her.

"Hi, neighbor!" She walked into his embrace,

kissing him. "What brings you to my end of the road this early?"

"You were on my mind a lot today." He grinned, squeezing her tight. "I picked up some steaks and veggies for skewers. How about after we grill those up, we take the boat out and watch the sunset from the water?" He kissed her forehead. "It'll be chilly once the sun goes down, so grab a sweater and jacket. Do you have those?"

It was a reminder that she'd only intended to be here another week or so. Even if she hadn't, she didn't have a lot of cold-weather clothes that she could have brought with her. If she was staying, she'd need to do some shopping.

"I have sweaters and a couple of wool blazers."

"Blazers? We're not going *yachting*, lady. I've got a spare jacket you can wear if you need it." Joey started barking from behind the door, apparently deciding his people had taken much too long to open the door and let him out. He leaped from the top of the steps to the ground in one long jump, then danced around Brittany's feet. Nate leaned over and scratched the pup's back, looking up to her. "So much for the stray that was never gonna be your dog, huh?"

Joey had his front paws on Nate's knee, looking at him adoringly. She watched them play together and smiled. Two unexpected males so deeply entrenched into her life. Two independent guys who were hers now. *Hers*. It was true. It was time to stop worrying about what might happen. Nate was hers and she'd fight to keep him. She'd make this work. No matter what.

They grilled dinner on Nate's deck, with the dog and cat hanging out nearby, just in case any bits of food were dropped. There was a hint of fall in the air, but it was still warm enough for them to eat out there, too. As Brittany sipped her wine, she had a vision of them sitting in that same spot in the future, maybe with a few children and dogs running around. Her sister might be visiting. Nate's mother and sister would be there. The lake would be shimmering in the sunshine. It would be their home. Their life. And it was right there, almost within her reach.

"Earth to Brittany?" Nate chuckled, taking her hand. "Where'd you go, babe?"

She blinked, her chest tight with emotion. "Honestly? I was imagining the future…our future." She looked into his eyes, warm and tender. "I want that, Nate. I want us to have a future together. I want to be *here* in the future." She straightened, realizing she'd been leaning toward him. "I mean…if that's what you want…"

Nate rose and pulled her into his arms, nuzzling his face in the hollow of her neck. His voice was rough and low.

"*If?* Do you really have any doubt, sweetheart? Of course I want you here." He took in a deep breath and raised his head to meet her gaze. "Brittany, I'm in love with you. I have been for a while now. I've just been careful… I didn't want to scare you away or make a fool of myself."

Her laughter bubbled up. "Oh, Nate. You couldn't scare me away if you tried. I love you, too. You must know that."

His eyes searched hers, suddenly serious. "*Do* you? Have I won your trust, Britt?"

"What? Of course! I'm trusting you with my heart, aren't I? And that's not something I do easily." She rested her hand on his cheek. "You have me heart and soul."

He opened his mouth as if to speak, then closed it again.

"What is it?"

He shook his head, his smile returning.

"Nothing. I'm sorry for asking so many questions when you just told me you love me. You *love* me. I'm the luckiest guy in the world." He kissed her lips, his mouth firm and demanding. She sighed, parting her lips to let him in. The kiss was different from any other of their kisses. It was full of…a future.

They stood there for a while, just clinging to each other and kissing. Then Nate ran his lips along her jaw, brushing them across the bottom of her ear.

"We need to get the boat out if we're going to catch that sunset."

They put dinner away and tucked Joey and Pepper in the house together. The dog and cat immediately jumped on the sofa, choosing opposite corners to curl up in. Nate dropped the wooden boat into the water and they headed out onto the glass-smooth lake just in time. He cut the engine when they reached the deep water. Without a breeze, he let the boat drift instead of dropping anchor. They sat together on the bench seat at the back of the boat, his arm over her shoulders and their heads touching. It was so quiet out there. No waves. Brittany snuggled closer to him.

That was what she hoped for their future. No waves. She just had to get through the next few weeks successfully.

"What are you going to do if you're living here?"

His question caught her off guard.

"Umm…well… I've got money set aside, so I won't be desperate." Her money would go a *lot* further in Gallant Lake than it would have in Tampa.

"But what about your sister? You're helping her, right?"

She pulled her head back and looked up at him.

"Are you trying to talk me out of this?"

He chuckled. "Never. But when we met, your goal seemed to be nothing short of world domination. I want to be sure you'll be happy here."

"I think I will." She felt him stiffen. "I mean, I *know* I'll be happy with you. As far as work goes, I'm sure there's always room for another real-estate agent." The sun was sinking behind the mountains, turning the sky brilliant shades of orange. "I could specialize

in lakefront property. Maybe even flip a few properties." She grinned. "You could help me furnish them
with funky antiques."

He nodded, relaxing a little.

"What about your friend?"

"What friend?"

"The guy you're property hunting for? Has he
made a decision yet?"

Her heart jumped. She wasn't ready for this conversation, and she sure as hell didn't want it right
after they declared their love for each other. Things
were too new. Too fragile.

"Uh...yeah... I mean...no, he hasn't decided.
He's...waffling on me. He may not buy anything at
this point. That's how some clients are." She quietly
crossed her fingers that was true. "The good news
is he brought me to Gallant Lake, right?"

Nate was quiet for a lot longer than Brittany was
comfortable with.

"Nate? Right?"

"Yeah, babe. That was good news." He kissed
the top of her head as the sun vanished completely.

The chill she felt was more than losing the sun's
warmth. He sounded disappointed, and she felt an
invisible wall growing between them. Did he know
something? Blake had sworn her to secrecy until he
had his end of the plan put together, so she was sure
he hadn't told Nate. But somehow, Nate seemed to

suspect something. Or maybe her guilt was making her paranoid.

She settled closer to him, and he gave her a reassuring squeeze.

"I love you, Britt."

That was enough. Love had to be enough. Because she couldn't keep secrets from him much longer.

Chapter Fourteen

Nate was still fighting to wake up on Monday morning when he opened the store. Hank blasted him with his curse words when he pulled the cover off the cage.

"I'm not in the mood, buddy."

Something in his tone must have rubbed Hank the wrong way, because he recited all of his X-rated words a second time. Nate tapped the cage to signal that playtime was over. Hank whistled, then yelled "Whatever, dude! Whatever, dude!"

Nate probably had Darius to thank for that new phrase. At least it wasn't offensive, so he let it go. He started a pot of coffee. He and Brittany had spent most of Saturday night, yesterday and last night between the sofa and his bed. Confessing their love had been a real turn-on for both of them, and they'd had lots of fun. She said she'd trusted him with her heart and soul. But she still didn't budge on telling him about her mysterious buyer friend. In fact, he was pretty sure she'd outright lied to him when she said the guy hadn't made a decision yet.

That didn't jibe with what Asher said about Louise having an offer. And *Stella* having an offer. Was this mystery man buying more than one business on Main Street? As terrific as every moment had been with Brittany that weekend, he still hadn't been able to shake all the questions from his head. He didn't want to doubt her. He wanted to believe she was all in. But she was holding back, and he didn't know why.

Louise came to the store shortly after he'd unlocked the front doors for business. She seemed agitated, and he brought her back to the office for a cup of coffee.

"What is it, Louise? What's up?"

Her eyes narrowed. "That's what I'd like to know, Nate. What's that girl of yours up to?"

"What do you mean?" His stomach dropped.

"I heard Stella got an offer from Brittany's 'friend.'" She made air quotes with her fingers. "And I also heard the Thompsons are thinking of accepting a verbal offer *they* got. And apparently it's raining offers from this guy, because guess what? *I* have an offer, too." Her back was ramrod straight. "We thought we were competing with each other. But we weren't. He wants *all* of our businesses. Have you had an offer, too?"

"No." He frowned. He'd told Brittany he had no interest in selling, but it seemed strange that she'd never brought him an offer. At this point, was he the only waterfront business that didn't have one?

Waterfront.

Brittany was a real-estate agent.

Buying up all the waterfront property in the middle of town for a *friend*.

His blood ran cold. It couldn't be. There had to be an explanation. She wouldn't do this. She wouldn't lie to him. Wouldn't lie to her friends in Gallant Lake. Wouldn't lie about *loving* him. Would she?

Louise was talking again. "…heard Sol Bernstein got an offer for the old firehouse, too. No one has contracts yet, but something's not right, Nate, and that girl of yours is in the middle of it."

"She's not my girl." Except…she was. He cleared his throat. "I'll look into it, but let's keep this between us for now, okay?" She started to object, but he talked over her. "I'm *not* protecting anyone, I swear. I just think there has to be a logical explanation for all of this. And if it goes public and creates panic for people, then we may never find out." He reached out to cover her hand on the desk. "You know me, Louise. You know I'd never do anything to hurt Gallant Lake. And I sure wouldn't sell the hardware that's been in my family since before the Civil War. You know that, right?"

"What if she's just seducing you to get her claws in the store?"

"That's bull." He sat back, hating that she'd just voiced the trace of a thought that had zipped across his mind like a meteor. "And it's exactly why I don't want you talking to people about this until we have *facts*. The conspiracy theories will spin out of control. Promise me, Louise. I mean it."

She studied him for a long time. Then her shoulders started to shake with laughter. "I've known you since you were a little kid with big ears and glasses who collected rocks. Rocks!"

He splayed his hands. "What can I say? I liked geology."

She chuckled. "You liked *rocks*. My point is, I've known you your whole life, and no one loves this town more than you do, except maybe Chief Dan Adams." Her smile faded. "But I also know you've been alone a long time. And this woman…"

"Before you say anything else, you need to know I'm in love with that woman."

Her eyebrows shot straight up. "You're in…" She shook her head. "Well, I'll be damned."

"Let me talk to her. You said no one has contracts yet, so maybe it's still some sort of competition thing, and the client is trying to play you all against each other. Brittany may not even know about it." He ignored the voice in his head telling him Brittany was too sharp not to know what was happening. "Let's not throw her under the bus just yet, okay?"

"Fine." Louise stood and grabbed her handbag from the floor. "I'll give you a week without me interfering. After that, I go to the mayor and the police chief." She hesitated at his office door. "But if I hear about any actual contracts coming through before that, our deal is off. I won't let my friends get ripped off."

"I don't think it's about that, but sure. If offers show up this week, you go public."

The problem was, he had no idea what this *was* about. And there was only one person who did.

Brittany opened the door of her cabin and felt all of her plans come crashing down around her feet.

"Conrad?" She stared at the two men on the wooden stoop. "Kent?"

The timing couldn't be worse. She was *so* close to putting a plan together with Blake. Now she had Nate asking questions and Conrad and his brown-nosing nephew standing on her doorstep. Why couldn't everyone give her the time she needed?

"Yes, Brittany. Conrad and Kent. I assume that was your way of inviting us in?"

He brushed past her without waiting for an answer, his nephew right behind him as always. Joey leaped off the sofa and barked wildly. Kent cursed under his breath, so she scooped up the dog with a fast apology and put him out back. She gathered as much composure as possible before turning to face them with what she hoped was a cool, confident smile.

"I'm sorry. I was just startled to find you here. You don't usually check up on me in the field, Conrad."

Kent, with his smoothed-down golden hair and slight build, wore a dark suit nearly identical to Conrad's. They both looked ridiculous dressed like that in a resort town. Kent's lip curled at her, and she wanted to slap him for the condescending look in his eye.

"Shouldn't you be addressing him as Mr. Quest?"

She didn't bother trying to keep the edge from her voice.

"I've been calling him by his first name since the time your teachers were calling you by yours in high school, Kent."

He opened his mouth to snap back, but Conrad raised his hand sharply to silence him.

"That's enough of that." He glared at Kent, giving Brittany a brief moment of hope that he wasn't here for trouble. A *very* brief moment. He turned to Brittany, his voice steely but level.

"It's true we've worked together a long time. And in all that time, I've never seen you take this long to find someone…anyone…willing to sell. I've never seen you avoid giving me progress reports…" She started to object, but he pushed on, grinding the words through his teeth now. "And I have *never* known you to try to change my mind about a plan. Or to outright *lie* to me."

She couldn't figure out how to respond. Deny the truth? Come clean? Stall him until she could talk to Blake? She took a long breath, forcing her hands to unclench and relax at her sides.

"I tried to get you to change your mind for *your* benefit, Conrad. When have I ever *not* had your best interests at heart?" She saw a flicker of doubt in his expression. "I've always been your barracuda. I've always worked to make the best deals for you, and you know it." More slight softening of his expression. "I've never seen a town like Gallant Lake, though." That was true, and it gave her the confidence to push ahead. "This town is all wrong for a Quest Properties project. I'm sorry, but that's the truth. They will fight, and they will drag this out in the courts. Even if they don't win, they'll slow the project and make it cost-prohibitive. That's why I suggested Connecticut…"

"Connecticut isn't going to happen. The viable communities around the casinos are fully saturated, and the casinos aren't doing that great right now. You'd know that if you did any actual research before suggesting it."

Kent picked at some lint…or dog hair…on his

sleeve. "Research a potential *partner* would know how to do."

The smarmy SOB had always had it out for her, jealous of her success when he could barely handle a residential closing without help from someone. And now he was gunning for her partnership. She held in a bitter laugh. He could *have* it.

"I'm telling you this town is different."

Joey barked at the door, and Conrad's eyes narrowed. "I think what's different is *you*. Since when have you had a dog?"

"Oh, uh…he was a stray and I adopted him. No big deal. Nothing to do with my work."

"I'm not so sure. And what's up with you making a unilateral decision to *not* include the hardware store?" He shook his head sadly. "I'm not an idiot, Brittany. I can Google things. Like the hardware's website and photos of its good-looking owner."

She couldn't argue about Nate being a gorgeous man. "I told you why—if we pick up the old firehouse, we'll have the same amount of space in a better location."

"How is it better when Nate Thomas's hardware store sits dead center of town, right next door to the town's park with walking access to the pier?"

"Exactly! You don't want to block that access. So starting at the next block of buildings makes more sense."

He stared at her, clearly unconvinced and downright angry. Joey yipped again, but she didn't want her small dog anywhere near these guys, so she left him outside. Conrad looked around the small cottage.

"I wonder if that mutt is the only thing you've picked up in this town." He nodded toward the kitchen counter, where two wineglasses were waiting to be washed. Ironically, it wasn't Nate she'd been drinking with. Mack had stopped by yesterday afternoon with a bottle of chardonnay and they'd each had a glass as they chatted about Dan getting the new police department up and running, and the wedding plans they were making for next year.

"You told me once that Gallant Lake was personal for you, Conrad." His eyes narrowed as she continued. "Well, it's personal for me, too. But I've offered good compromises for you. And I didn't lie when I said this town will fight you with everything they've got." And she'd be standing by their sides. "It's just not a good fit for Quest Properties."

His voice was cool. "Because people won't sell?"

She raised her hands. "Exactly!"

"Before you dig any deeper, you need to know that I stopped by and had a chat with Louise Di-Angelo before I came here. Turns out she's had a so-called 'verbal offer' on her business but hasn't seen an actual contract yet. Said she's not the only one." He took a menacing step forward. "What the hell is going on, Brittany? Why haven't I seen any of these agreements? Why haven't we processed purchase offers to get them on record before values jump? What are you playing at?"

She wanted to tell him to take a hike. Literally. A long hike off a short dock, as Nate liked to say. But she couldn't blow this up yet. For one thing, she had a contract with Conrad dictating the terms of her employment. For another, she had to give Blake time to put his plan together.

She spread her hands in confession.

"You've got me, Conrad. I have put the brakes on a few deals while I tried to change your mind. But none of those deals are dead, just on hold. I'd like you to…"

"I don't give a flying fu—" He took a deep breath. "I don't care what you'd like me to do. Get those contracts signed this week or I'll send Kent out to get them signed for you. And you'll be unemployed. Got it?"

Conrad turned toward the door. Kent followed, giving her another sneer.

"Let's face it," Kent said. "You're already unemployed when this is over. But if you don't fix this, we'll sue you, Doyle. You'll lose your real-estate license. You'll be finished in Tampa." He moved so close that she had no choice but to lean away, hating to give him the satisfaction. His breath was rank against her skin. "You'll be finished everywhere."

And just like that, she'd had enough.

"You know what?" She stepped forward so that

her chest bumped against his, and not in a flirta-
tious way. She glared down at him. "I'm already finished." Her gaze moved to Conrad. "I'm done doing
your dirty work, and I'm sure as *hell* not going to be
pushed around by this little pissant nephew of yours."
She took a turn at sneering. "Good luck getting anywhere in Gallant Lake. You might pick up a shop or
two, but you'll never get enough. Not with me leading the fight against you."

Conrad's face grew red. "You can't afford to quit
and we both know it. You're supporting your sister,
remember?"

She went very still, her rage turning her into a
warrior carved of granite. "Not that my sister is any
of your business, but she graduates next year and
has made it clear she does not want or need my as-
sistance. I'm not kidding, Conrad. I'm done."

Conrad yanked the front door open on his way
out, barking orders over his shoulder as if she hadn't
just quit. Kent was trotting at his uncle's heels. Probably trying to figure out how to literally get his head
completely up his ass.

"Do the job I'm paying you for, Doyle," Conrad
said, "and get those contracts in my hands this week.
Including one from your boyfriend. I'm building those
condos, with or without you."

The door slammed shut behind them so loudly
that she jumped, even though she'd watched them
slam it. Conrad's arrival was a complication. It was

probably going to move up her timeline. She still had no idea if she was going to have a job with Blake or not. Kent would be trying to roadblock her every move because he'd want to be the one to swoop in and save the deal for his uncle. That was why Conrad had tossed that *with or without you* threat. But those were all minor details compared to her only priority. Nate.

She was letting Joey in the back door when there was a sharp rap on her front door. Conrad probably wanted to yell a few more orders at her to show off in front of Kent. Rolling her eyes, she pulled it open.

"Yes, boss, I heard you. Bilk the old folks out of their properties so you can build those butt-ugly condo…" Her voice trailed off. Funny how impossible it was to speak when your lungs emptied and refused to work.

It wasn't Conrad outside her door. It was Nate. And he *knew*. She could tell from the tightness in his jaw and the cold look in his eyes. His mouth—that beautiful mouth that had skimmed her body from head to toe last night—was pressed in a thin, angry line. She didn't know how. But Nate knew.

"Oh…" She started to paint a smile on her face, but it felt wrong and she gave it up. She had no idea what he'd heard or from whom. "Uh…hi, Nate. I… wasn't expecting you."

"I'll bet you weren't." He brushed past her, barely acknowledging Joey's excited greeting. He stared out the window, back to her, and raked his fingers through his hair, leaving it standing on end. "Was any of it real, Britt?"

"I… What do you mean?" Without knowing how much he knew, she didn't want to say something that would get her in even more trouble. He *loved* her. He'd said so. A lot. Since the boat ride, they'd been declaring their love for each other practically every ten minutes. Oh, God. He was asking if her *love* was real. Her heart cracked clean in two.

"You need to know that whatever else you're thinking, I absolutely love you."

He dropped his head, his voice so low she could barely hear him.

"I don't think I want your love."

"Don't *say* that!" Her voice broke. "We can fix whatever's happened." She started to beg. "Whatever you've heard, whatever you *think*, there's more to it. It's not what it might sound like…"

Her usually gentle Nate spun on his heel so quickly that she jumped back. His face was red with rage, his voice rough and bitter.

"Really? Are you going to tell me you didn't just say you were bilking old people out of their properties? Old people like my *friends*? Like Stella? And Louise? Bob and Sue? And maybe even Sol, who I didn't even know you knew? Tell me how *that* isn't what I think."

"I'm not… That's not what I…" His fury had her off balance, and she had to take a breath to slow her adrenaline. He knew more than she'd thought, but she had to stay calm. It hurt that he could believe that of her so quickly. But there was time to turn this around. She just needed to get Nate to listen. Then she needed to call Blake Randall before *everything* blew sky-high.

"Nate, look at me." His eyes narrowed on her. She put her hands on her hips. "Don't *glare* at me. *Look* at me. I'm the same woman you took out on your boat Saturday night and confessed your love to. I told you I love you, too."

He scoffed. "Only after I said it. Maybe you just played me."

"How can you say that?" She breathed the question more than said it, wincing from the pain of his accusation. "Look, I know you're angry, but I'm not bilking anyone. I promise. And I didn't lie to you. I love you, Nate. You know me. You know I'm telling you the truth."

"Are you saying you've always told me the truth?"

She couldn't help it. She hesitated.

"That's what I thought." He smirked, but there was no humor in it. If anything, it was even worse than his look of rage. He was dismissing her, heading for the door. She reached for him but he jerked away. And that was when she snapped. She'd expected anger. And hurt. But she'd never dreamed he'd just…drop her like trash. Like her mother's family had when they were homeless and afraid. A swell of righteous anger rose in her.

"How dare you!" He turned when her voice rose. "You're just tossing me aside? We fell in *love*. And just like that, you're done with me. Without even listening." She walked toward him. "I'm starting to wonder how real *your* love was, Nate. Because if someone told me something horrible about you, even if they had the receipts, I would be ready to *fight* them right then and there. Because I know you. The real you. Or at least, I thought I did." She waved her finger in his face. "But you didn't treat me any better just now than those bastards in Tampa when I was a kid. Like I was garbage."

His face went slack, his anger suspended for the moment. "No. It's not like that, Britt. I…"

"Well, it *feels* just like that. And that sucks." She hit her chest with the palm of her hand. Her words tumbled out. "I screwed up. Well, I didn't screw up. I came here to do my job, which I'm good at. But then I fell in love with this place. And with you. I screwed up by not telling you the whole truth, but I was under contract. I was trying to fix everything before I told you. For us." Tears welled up in her eyes. "But if you can turn on me this fast… I'm wondering why I even bothered."

"Brittany…"

She waved him off. "You should leave."

"I *was* leaving. Look, I don't want you feeling

like I'm discarding you, but you lied to me. Under contract or not, that's a deal-breaker when you're supposed to be in love with me. I knew you were holding something back, but I had no idea that *something* involved my town. My business. My friends."

"They're my friends, too!" she shouted. But would that be true once the news got out?

He shook his head, letting out a long, slow sigh.

"It's not like I'm just listening to random gossip here. I *heard* your boss when he left. He told you to get the sales contracts so he can build condos. And *you're* the one who said you were bilking old people."

That explained the extra edge to his anger. He'd been outside when Conrad and Kent left. That had to have looked and sounded pretty damn bad. But they were way beyond her trying to explain that at this point. They'd both said things that would be hard to take back.

She gestured toward the door, suddenly exhausted and so very sad.

"I think you and I need to just…stop talking. Seriously. Just go."

His eyes closed.

"I don't want us to…"

"Go."

They stared at each other, standing a good four or five feet apart. It may as well have been the Grand Canyon.

He turned away and opened the door. "You need

to know that I won't let this happen. Whatever your employer is up to in Gallant Lake, I'll stop it. I'll stop *you*."

It was almost funny. He was vowing to stop her, even though she'd said she was fixing things. She didn't bother pointing out that contradiction. They'd blown past the point of having a real conversation about things. Her chin rose, and her old defenses rose up.

"I told you they call me The Barracuda, remember? You won't stop me."

He chewed on the inside of his cheek, his body rigid. But he didn't reply.

He just walked away.

Chapter Fifteen

"I don't know, man. That doesn't sound like something Brittany would do. I mean, she's been in my home. Had dinner with Mack and me." Dan Adams folded his arms across his chest, leaning against the door frame of Nate's office. He was in uniform, although he'd tossed his hat on the desk. "She let my ten-year-old daughter teach her how to do some dance that's hot on TikTok right now. And haven't you…like…*slept* with the woman?" Dan tipped his head to the side. "And you're buying into Louise's story?"

Nate stared up at the ceiling, chewing his lip and trying to ignore the growing voice in his head saying he was making a huge mistake.

"How can I *not* believe it, Dan? Four businesses— five counting me—received purchase offers yester- day. Hand-delivered by that Kent asshole."

He scowled at the memory of the smug little blond bastard in the custom-cut suit strolling in yesterday like he already owned the freaking place. Appar- ently, Brittany was too ashamed to present him with her boss's offer herself.

"Exactly," Dan said. "The offer came from that guy, *not* Brittany."

"The guy she *works* for. Maybe she just didn't have the guts to look me in the eye."

Dan sighed. "Yeah? So why didn't she have the guts to face Stella? Or Louise? She didn't deliver *any* of the offers, Nate. Not a one. Kent Quest—which is a comic book name if I ever heard one—handed out all the offers yesterday afternoon. I thought you were falling for Brittany, man. Why are you so eager to throw her under the bus?"

Nate stood and started pacing the small office. "I *was* falling for her. I *did* fall for her. It felt so damn real. But what if she was just using me? What if it was a sham?"

"What if it wasn't?"

Nate stopped and turned. "Do you know some- thing I don't?"

"No!" Dan threw up his hands. "That's my point. I have more faith in your woman than *you* do, and that's fu…" Dan glanced back at Hank, knowing the bird would repeat that word for an hour if he heard it. "That's screwed up. And now you're involved in this community meeting tonight. To what end?"

The meeting had actually been Louise's idea, and the mayor had agreed yesterday to put out a notice for an emergency meeting of the town council, open to the public. Stella had asked Nate to speak. He'd be standing in front of the local population, arguing against Brittany and her employer, Quest Properties.

That news had come out earlier in the week, when someone recognized Conrad Quest. Nate had looked him up online and had read how the company made their profits from buying up chunks of land and building concrete condos and shopping plazas in small towns on the outskirts of growing cities. Quest's nephew, Kent, had agreed to speak at the meeting to address people's "concerns."

He glanced at Dan, then lowered his eyes, not feeling all that proud of himself.

"I told her I'd stop this, and I meant it. We can change the zoning. We can call for environmental impact studies. We can stop Brittany and her boss from destroying our town."

"What the hell is *wrong* with you?" Dan asked. "Why are you taking up pitchforks against your own girlfriend?"

"Don't call her that. Remember, I've been lied to before."

"Are you talking about your *dad*? Come on, Nate.

This is not the same thing as your dad almost gambling away the store."

"My father told me everything was going to be fine. Told me not to worry. That it wasn't what it looked like. That he'd fix it." Nate shook his head. "All the same things Brittany told me on Monday. Word for word. I *believed* Dad and we nearly lost this place. I'm still digging out of the debt from that loan I had to take." He gestured around at the walls and the lake outside the window. "I barely managed to save this. And now I find the woman I love might be trying to take it away again?"

"*Might* be." Dan, ever the investigator, picked up on every detail. "You don't know. You're not sure. Have you *asked* her if that's what she's doing?"

"She denied it, but she'd do that anyway, right?"

"Wow." Dan shook his head slowly back and forth. "Mack was right—you're just tossing Britt to the curb, aren't you?"

The phrasing struck Nate like a sledgehammer. She'd accused him of discarding her like trash. "Has Mack been talking to Brittany? Have you?"

"I think the bigger question is…have *you*?"

"Hard to do after she threw me out of her place."

"Three days ago. You drive by there every time you go home." Dan reached for his hat. "Let me ask you something. Is this pile of bricks really more important than your feelings for Brittany?"

He didn't understand the question. "This business has been in my family for…"

"Five generations. Yeah, I know. Everyone in town knows. Is *that* more important than Brittany Doyle?" Dan squared his hat on his head and ran his fingers along the brim. "In other words, are you okay with losing *her* and keeping *this*?"

He thought of coming into the store day after day for the rest of his life without seeing Brittany up on the ladder stocking nails, or teaching Hank new insults, or sitting on his desk giving Nate that come-do-me look. Dan was still talking.

"Just saying that, once upon a time, I thought my relationship with Mack interfered with my job and that she was bad for me. And then I lost her. And almost *really* lost her when she stumbled onto that drug warehouse out at Gilford's Ridge. That was when I realized my job—my *life*—was meaningless without Mackenzie Wallace in it." Dan shrugged. "Instead of focusing on how butt-hurt you are that Brittany didn't tell you everything, maybe focus on what matters. Is your life better with her or without her?"

Dan turned and left without waiting for an answer, having a brief whistling competition with Hank on his way to the door. Nate stood at the window for close to an hour, hands in his pockets, replaying his entire relationship with Brittany in his head. The laughs. The debates. The sex. The barns explored. The sunsets shared. The love.

Something started to break loose inside him. Dan said he was focusing on being hurt. *Hurt.* Was that what triggered his angry reaction to what was happening? Were his feelings wrapped up in memories of his father, instead of the reality of what he and Brittany had together? She'd said he was tossing her aside like trash, and he thought of the stories she'd told of her past. Living on the streets. Rummaging for food, and vowing to protect her little sister no matter what. That was why she worked so hard, clawing for every penny she could get to protect Ellie and make sure neither of them would want for anything.

Brittany was tough as nails. But she was also more fragile than anyone knew. She told him she'd have fought anyone who had the nerve to accuse him of anything suspicious. But he'd readily believed the worst about her. Even though he had his doubts that she could have done it, he'd ignored those doubts and jumped all over her. He thought about how that would make that little homeless girl feel—to be accused of something she didn't do. He dropped his head, his knees almost buckling under the weight of what he'd done. He gripped the windowsill to steady himself.

He'd hurt the only woman he'd ever loved. Because he didn't trust his own intuition? Because he'd been betrayed in the past? It didn't matter why. He'd been wrong to flip out so quickly, to push her away instead of listening. She kept saying she was trying to fix things. He hoped she still believed *they* were worth fixing.

The emergency meeting announcement had received so many responses that the town board moved it to the grade school gymnasium to make room for everyone who wanted to attend. The echoing sound of a few hundred people talking and going up and down the old bleachers made Brittany's headache even worse than it had been. She'd hardly slept this week, and never for more than an hour or two at a time. Her daylight hours had been spent on the phone when she wasn't meeting with Blake Randall at the resort.

She'd avoided going into Gallant Lake. For one thing, she didn't know if she could handle seeing Nate. Not when she knew he'd turned on her along with the rest of the people in town. Louise had been very busy spreading all sorts of stories about Brittany's role in Quest coming here, and what they were up to. In a few versions of the conspiracy, Brittany was the mastermind of it all, looking to bulldoze everything in town and turn it all into a parking lot. She was Cruella de Vil in the flesh. A "money-grubbing she-devil who didn't care about anyone in this town."

Those last words were a direct quote from Louise, who'd confronted her on Wednesday when she'd tried to get a cup of coffee and get a gauge of what people were thinking. It was far worse than she'd imagined. So much so that, after Louise confronted her on the sidewalk in front of a small but angry crowd, she'd retreated to her car and gone home.

She'd had a few voice mails and texts from Nora and Mack, but she hadn't even opened them. In fact, she'd left her phone almost exclusively facedown. She didn't think she could bear seeing or hearing her friends accusing her of destroying Gallant Lake, too. She got it—everyone hated her. After tonight's meeting, they might feel differently, but it wouldn't matter. The damage had been done. She was leaving. She'd already booked her flight from JFK to Tampa.

Turned out small towns could turn on you just as fast as city streets could. Even Nate had been more protective of himself than of their love for each other. She sniffed. Let them have their stupid little town and let him keep all his dumb antiques. She'd start fresh somewhere and remember her personal golden rule: never mix friendship and business. In fact, forget friendship. Forget love. Just find a job and make a living. If she needed friends or lovers, she could always read a book.

Someone's hand brushed hers and she flinched away. Her trust levels were at a lifelong low. Nora Peyton gave her a sad smile.

"Sorry. It's just me. How have you been?"

She blinked away the rush of tears. No one had

asked her that question this week. She reminded herself that she was used to people not caring.

"I'm fine."

Nora laughed. "O-kay. That sounded about as un-fine as anything I've ever heard, but if that's what you're going with tonight, it's okay by me." Her laughter faded. "I've called you a couple of times. Did you get my messages?"

"I think my inbox is full." The truth was she'd left her phone facedown for two days now. She felt brittle, as if she'd shatter at the slightest touch. "When you've heard one insult, you've heard them all, you know?"

She'd had dozens of messages from random strangers the first day, calling her names. There was even a veiled threat from some guy who'd sounded drunk—*we know where you live*.

"No, I don't know," Nora said. "Has someone been bothering you?"

She shook her head sharply, not wanting to discuss it. She just wanted to get through this meeting and get away. The mayor stepped to the microphone and asked everyone to take a seat. Brittany looked at the typewritten agenda in her hand, her eyes blurring at the name of the third scheduled speaker. Nate Thomas.

I'll stop you.

He must hate her so much. The thought made her shoulders slump. She'd expected him to be there, but seeing him sitting in the first row, only three seats from Conrad, made her chest go tight. He looked tired. And sad. She knew the feeling.

Conrad was first on the agenda, and he stood to a loud round of booing. He smiled and raised his hand, trying to silence them as if they were children. It didn't work. Dan Adams had to step forward from the corner where he'd been standing. His stern look was enough to settle everyone.

Conrad was just as smooth as ever, apologizing for "misunderstandings" created by his former employee—that would be her—and trying to assure everyone that despite the way his plans had been "misrepresented" by some, he had Gallant Lake's best interests at heart. He talked demographics and New York City and seasonal resort statistics and property values and fairness, and it all blended into the sound of a tuba played by a six-year-old in Brittany's head.

But he had attractive graphics and videos, and when he talked money, a few people started to sit up and listen. Until he displayed the artist's rendering of the waterfront condos and offices he wanted to build along Main Street. There was a collective gasp in the gymnasium when the modern monstrosity showed up on the screen, twelve feet tall.

Ever nimble, he quickly added that the plans were just a "first stab" at the design, and it could be changed. All Brittany could think was that she'd like to take a first stab at *him*. Conrad wrapped up his pitch by again apologizing for *her* and promising to move forward with complete transparency. *That would be a first.*

Louise rose to her feet slowly, leveling a malevolent glare at Conrad as she passed him. She talked passionately about the legacy of the waterfront businesses, without mentioning that hers was struggling, just like most of the others. She talked about the waterfront being the town's finest asset, and that covering it with ugly condos was a desecration. Brittany couldn't argue there. Then she lifted her head and stared straight at Brittany, standing as close to the exit as possible without being outside. She braced herself when Louise pointed her out, everyone turning toward her. Her hand slid behind her, resting on the door's push bar. She could be out of here in a flash.

"And then *this* girl comes to town and starts stealing our properties! Buildings that have been in our families for generations!" An angry grumble went across the room like a wave. Brittany gripped the door more tightly. Nate stood, and she leaned back, cracking the door open fractionally. She couldn't stand here and listen to him join in the pile-on. It would destroy her to hear him attacking her. He held up his arms to quiet the room. Louise looked smug, as if she knew exactly what was coming.

"Hold on, everyone." He'd said he didn't like public speaking, but his voice right now commanded attention, even though Louise still had the microphone. "For one thing, Brittany Doyle is *not* a *girl*. She's a professional woman, and she came here to do the job her boss demanded of her." He glared at Conrad. Was Nate…? Was he *defending* her? Brittany's heart skipped. Not finished, Nate walked over and took the mic.

"And I'd like to know exactly why you think she 'stole' anything." He turned to Louise. "Your building's been for sale for over a year. You said you were retiring. You got a fair offer. You accepted it. How is that *theft*?" The woman's mouth opened and closed as she huffed and blustered. Nate turned away from her. "Sol's owned the old firehouse for five years. Remember when he told us he was going to convert it into a restaurant? It's sat there empty since he bought it, and it's been on the market for three years."

Someone shouted from the audience. "What about the hardware, Nate? Did you have *that* on the market?"

"No. And Brittany never made me an offer on it. That's my point." He stole a quick glance toward the back of the room, where she stood, but she couldn't read his expression. "No one is forcing anyone to do anything."

"But she *did* lie," Louise said. "She lied to all of us."

Nate turned to her. "Did she? She told you she was looking at commercial property for an investor." He gestured toward Conrad. "That was true."

"But…" Louise hesitated. "She went around pretending to be our friend while she was doing all this. She pretended to be your *girl*friend. How can you defend her?"

Brittany held her breath, wanting the answer to that question more than anyone here. But he didn't answer Louise directly.

"I don't know what's true or not true any more than you do." His forehead wrinkled as if he was struggling with himself. "That's my point. Since when has this been a town that turns on someone without knowing the facts? It's not what we're about. It's not what *I'm* about." He rubbed the back of his neck, scowling at the floor for a long moment. Then he looked up at the bleachers, where everyone was sitting. "What if Brittany *wasn't* pretending?"

He turned his head to stare at her, and she wasn't prepared for the power of his eyes meeting hers directly. She felt the heat from his gaze. The anger. The hurt. The conflict. With a rush, she realized he *wanted* to believe her. He *wanted* her to be telling the truth. To be in love with him. It wasn't everything. It wasn't as if he was taking her at her word, and that still hurt. But knowing that he *wanted* to believe was something.

Someone shouted out another question, and Nate turned away from her.

The door opened behind Brittany so quickly she almost tumbled right out of it. Blake Randall caught her by the shoulders and saved her the embarrassment. Amanda was right behind him. Blake looked around as he stepped inside, muttering an expletive under his breath. He glanced at Brittany.

"Am I too late? Have they done anything?"

She gave him a wry smile. "Other than trying to decide whether to tar and feather me or simply ride me out of town on a rail? No, not much."

"And which side is Nate on?" Amanda reached out to squeeze Brittany's arm.

"So far he seems opposed to actual hot tar. He's sort of playing peacemaker."

"Good. Let's go." Blake's arm slid around her waist, pulling her along as he headed to the gym floor.

"Wait! No…"

But it was too late. She was being swept along toward the podium, where Nate was speaking.

"…don't want those condos any more than you do. I don't *know* Conrad Quest and I sure as hell don't *like* him. But there's no reason to burn Brittany at the same time. We don't know her involvement…"

She cringed. That was far from a glowing endorsement, considering the number of times she'd slept in that man's arms. But it was better than the angry words they'd thrown at each other on Monday.

Blake's voice called out right next to her.

"*I* know her involvement! She's worked her ass off to actively prevent those condos from being built."

Nate spun to face them. His eyes narrowed when he saw Blake's arm around her. Blake must have noticed, because he released her immediately. These two men had been on opposing sides in Gallant Lake before, when Nate led the fight to keep Blake from building a casino there. Blake stepped up to Nate, leaning in and saying something in Nate's ear. Nate gave him the microphone. He didn't stand by Brittany, though. Instead, he went to the opposite side of the podium. She raised her chin, refusing to show how much it hurt.

Blake introduced himself, as if everyone in Gallant Lake didn't know the largest employer in town. She looked at Conrad, and his face was scarlet with rage. Blake clearly hadn't told her the whole story between the two men. This kind of anger didn't come from some lost business deal.

"Since there seems to be a rush to judgment when it comes to Brittany Doyle, let me start by saying the only reason you all *won't* have to fight Conrad Quest and his plans is because Brittany made sure they wouldn't happen." Another murmur went through the room, but it didn't sound as angry as before. "And the only reason Quest is here at all is because of me." Silence fell on the gymnasium. "As ridiculous as it sounds, this mess started back at Harvard. I won't bore you with all the details, but Conrad and I have been competing for a very long time. For girls. For grades. For properties. And I've won most of those battles. Quest looked at the Gallant Lake Resort before I bought it. He didn't pull the trigger fast enough, but I did. When my father and brother tried to take it from me, it was Quest who was backing them financially. He tried to build his *own* casino on the lake, and I blocked that, too."

Louise stood and glared at Conrad. "Are you kidding me? You created this mess because of some personal vendetta? Maybe our police chief needs to lock you up." Everyone's head swiveled to Dan Adams. He looked to Blake, who shook his head.

"He's not a psycho stalker. I'm sure he's been careful to do all this by the book. He could have made plenty of money, because he's right—Gallant Lake needs long-term vacation homes and rentals. And *I'm* going to build them."

Another ripple of reaction moved through the meeting. People looked confused. Louise folded her arms on her chest.

"So how does that make *you* any better than *him*?"

Blake placed his hand over his heart. "Because I'm not building them in the center of town. I'm not coming after your properties, because I've owned the perfect property all along. It surrounds the golf course and runs along the lakeshore. It's part of the parcel I added to the resort five years ago." He glanced toward Brittany. "My thing is hotels, so I wasn't sure how to develop or market condos. But Brittany Doyle does. Let me introduce the new vice president of sales and rentals for our planned Gallant Lake Resort Waterfront Villas. Pending environmental impact studies, we've been assured permits shouldn't be a problem."

Blake leveled a hard stare at Conrad, who looked like he was gonna burst a blood vessel right then and there. "You like to be the big dog in town, Conrad. I'm guessing your appetite for condos in Gallant Lake is already fading. After all, you'd be competing with condos on the grounds of the hottest resort in the Catskills. And they'll be mine."

A roar of applause rose in the gymnasium. There was a rush of people around Brittany and Blake, clapping her on the back and smiling. Even a few apologies mixed in. Then a hand gripped her arm firmly and turned her.

Conrad ground his words through his teeth. "You signed a noncompete clause in your contract, and I could take you to court for going to work for Randall. You know that, right?"

"Yes, I'm aware. But those things can be tricky to enforce in court. You *might* be able to show that Blake Randall is a competitor, but I won't be working for Blake. I'm opening a real-estate office of my own here in Gallant Lake, so I won't be competing with you unless you're suddenly interested in selling rural family farms."

The lies still came too easily to her lips, but she didn't want to ruin Blake's big moment. Staying had been the plan. No one had to know just yet that she'd decided to leave. Staying here would be impossible when she'd have to see Nate all the time and know that he'd set her aside.

Conrad's brows rose. "You? The *Barracuda* is going to sell farms here in the middle of nowhere? And what about Randall's condos?"

She lifted her shoulder. "What about them? Once they're finally built, which will be long after the non-compete clause expires, it makes sense for a local Realtor to manage sales and rentals, right?" It made her sad to think that it wouldn't be her, but Blake would find someone. She leaned forward, lowering her voice. "This barracuda is leaving the deep waters to you. Have fun out there, Conrad."

She turned away, feeling a strange mix of sorrow and satisfaction. The town had been saved. But the cost had been high. She searched the faces for Nate, not sure why she was looking. To forgive him? To see if he'd forgiven her? It didn't matter. He wasn't there.

Chapter Sixteen

Nate walked from the school to the store, where his van was parked. The air was sharp and cool—his favorite kind of autumn night. A full moon was just coming up over Gallant Mountain, soft and peachy. Unlike his life right now, which was the polar opposite of peachy.

He'd left the gymnasium before the meeting was even finished. Once Blake Randall made his big speech and told the truth about what Brittany had been up to behind the scenes, Nate couldn't stay in the room another minute. He'd vowed to fight her, and she'd already been fighting for everything he believed in. The problem was…he hadn't believed in *her*.

"Stop! Police! Freeze, asshole!" Hank started hollering as soon as Nate unlocked the shop door. He understood the bird's confusion, since he'd already been fed and covered for the night. Nate turned on just one bank of lights so the bird wouldn't be too freaked out, then pulled off the cage cover and tossed him a banana chip.

Hank let out a string of whistles and alarm sounds but settled down once he grabbed the chip from his dish. His sounds became more like contented chirps than shrieks.

"Sorry, buddy. Didn't mean to scare you. I just don't want to go home right now." Nate sat on a nearby barrel. He had no idea what to do with himself. Driving past Brittany's cabin would be like stabbing himself in the chest. Walking into his house, so full of memories… He looked at the office door. He could always sleep on the old cot he had in there. He sighed, talking to Hank. "Can I keep you company, pal?"

In response, Hank let out a string of obscenities. Nate didn't bother tapping the cage. He let the bird say them over and over. If anyone deserved to be cussed out right now, it was him.

"You know, I think there might be a law against that language in a public place." Dan Adams closed the door behind him as he stepped inside. "You okay in here?"

"Stop! Intruder! Police!" The parrot started as soon as he heard Dan's voice.

The police chief glared at him. "I *am* the police, you dumb bird."

"Whatever, dude. Whatever, dude. Whatever, dude."

Dan chuckled, leaning against the rack of chain and rope. "Seriously, Nate. You looked a little pale when you booked outta there. You didn't see that coming, huh?"

"Did *you*? Did you know about what Brittany and Blake had cooked up?"

Dan shook his head. "I wouldn't have let you beat yourself up earlier if I had. I mean, I guess I'd heard about Blake getting the go-ahead on adding more buildings, but that was a year ago, and nothing ever happened." Dan's phone buzzed. He checked it, tapped something into it, then slid it back in his pocket. "Just Mack asking if I'd be home before Chloe went to bed." His head tipped to the side. "Shouldn't you be a little happier right now? Downtown Gallant Lake is safe. I saw Quest and his nephew booking it out of town on my way over here. And your girl—excuse me, your *woman*—isn't the devil after all. So why do you look like someone stole your puppy?"

Nate stared at the floor. Hank had finally settled down, so the store was silent. The air was heavy with all the familiar smells—wood, dust, age, history. It had been in his family for… He shook his head.

Dan was right—he said that a lot. Was he using it as a crutch, as Brittany had accused him of a while back? A way to cling to the familiar and never have to take a risk?

"Nate?"

He flinched, almost forgetting Dan was sitting there.

"Sorry. I'm thinking about what you asked earlier. If this place was more important than Brittany." He looked around again. "And the answer is no. Nothing is more important than her. But she doesn't know that. I didn't trust her, Dan. After she told me she loved me, I just…" He thought of the pain in her eyes as she stood in the center of the cabin. "I made her feel like she'd been tossed aside. She's been treated like she was disposable her whole damn life, and instead of being her refuge, I acted just like everyone else and…"

The shop door opened again. Asher Peyton stepped in. Why hadn't he locked that damn door? Hank ruffled his feathers and whistled. Asher, who knew him even better than Dan did, stared at Nate in silence before shaking his head.

"You really fu…" He glanced at Hank. "I mean *screwed* things up with Brittany, didn't you?"

"Pretty Britt-ney! Pretty Britt-ney!" Of all the times for Hank to decide to attempt Brittany's name. There was a hush in the store. The bird repeated it again, until Asher tapped the cage to stop him.

"Hank, that is *cold*. Don't be a bully." Asher dropped some parrot treats into the dish, and Hank was immediately distracted by the crunchy food.

"To answer your question," Dan started, "yes, Nate screwed up. And he seems to think this little pity party will help somehow. Did you bring booze?"

Asher slid his hands into his pockets and rocked back on his heels, considering his words before speaking.

"You're the one with keys to the liquor store right across the street. Why don't you go grab us a bottle. From the looks of this guy, we're gonna be here awhile."

Dan stood. "Good plan. Be right back."

Once he left, Asher pulled a few boxes of paint over and sat down next to Nate, extending his legs out in front of him. Silence fell on the store.

"It's never hopeless." Asher's voice was low, but emphatic. "Even when you think it might be. It never is. Not unless you give up."

"I don't know, Ash." The future was yawning before him like a dark chasm.

A few more minutes of silence.

"I *do* know. If she's worth fighting for, then effing do it."

Dan came through the door, brandishing a bottle in his hand.

"Has he cried yet? I haven't missed seeing him cry, have I?"

"Screw you, Mr. Police Chief." Nate reached for the bottle with his first near-smile of the day. His friends weren't panicking, which helped *him* stop panicking. He felt a flicker of hope starting to burn in his chest.

Asher knew where Nate kept the glasses in his office, and he brought out three, along with a chair. He grinned as he slid the chair toward Dan.

"Does this bring back memories?"

Dan sat and took a glass. "Are you referring to the night I stopped you from drinking yourself into a stupor and helped you get your head out of your ass?" He chuckled as Nate filled their glasses. "We may be going at this backward right now. He's sober and we're gettin' him drunk."

"But we're still helping him get his head out of his ass, so it's okay." Asher held his glass up. "Whatever works."

Nate closed his eyes and focused on the burn of the whiskey going down before speaking.

"What the hell are you guys talking about?"

Asher reminded Nate that when he and Nora first met and fell in love, it was while Nora's daughter and Asher's son were about to have a baby. Asher had lost a son years before, and he didn't handle the news well. He and Nora were head over heels for each other, until Asher panicked and left her. His buddy Dan went up to Asher's half-finished mountain home and found him there, trying to dull his pain with alcohol. Dan had given him a firm talking-to, got him dried out and gave him a kick in the butt to go get Nora back.

"I appreciate this story, guys, but…" Nate still couldn't see how to get Brittany back. "I made more than just a mistake. I didn't trust her. And before you wave that off, you gotta know this—she grew up hard. Homeless a lot of the time. Living out of a car with her mom and her little sister. She's been treated like hell by a lot of people. And now by me."

His friends digested that for a minute. Dan frowned. "That explains her drive to succeed. A past like that will chase you for a long damn time."

"Exactly." Nate drained his glass and refilled it. "Now I have to win her trust all over again."

Asher held his glass out for a refill, and Nate obliged. Asher lifted the glass in a mock toast.

"So go do it, man. Stop feeling sorry for yourself and fix it. Crawl and beg if you have to. But fix it. You'll never forgive yourself if you don't."

Dan declined another drink, setting his glass down on the floor by his feet. "I agree. Do whatever you have to do. But don't do it tonight. You're on your way to the bottom of that bottle, and that's not all bad. As long as you don't plan on driving anywhere."

He shook his head. "I'm staying here tonight. I can't handle the house right now."

"Okay. Stay here. Enjoy the whiskey. Get some sleep. Tomorrow you can come up with a plan."

Someone was pounding on the store doors. Nate sat bolt straight, blinking and trying to get his bearings. He'd killed the bottle of whiskey last night. He regretted doing that before he'd set up the cot, but it was only a minor struggle. The store was warm enough that he didn't need blankets. He just fell onto it fully dressed and passed out. He squinted at his watch. It wasn't even seven thirty.

Hank was just as startled as Nate was, screaming "Son of a bitch!" over and over as Nate staggered out to the shop. He pulled off Hank's cage cover as he went by, earning him a few more choice words from the bird. Nate stopped when he saw who was on the other side of the door. Asher and Nora. Nora pounded again.

"Okay! Okay!" Nate unlocked the door and Nora grabbed his arm, not bothering with a greeting.

"Did you mean what you told Asher last night? That you want Brittany back?"

Nate looked at Asher, who just shrugged. "She's my wife. I tell her everything."

"Yes, Nora. I meant it."

"Well then, you'd better get moving. Because she's leaving today. She's got a flight out of JFK this afternoon."

Nate was wide-awake now.

"What do you mean, she's *leaving*? She's got a job with Blake Randall…all those condos…"

Nora gave a sharp shake of her head. "No. She told Blake after the meeting that she can't stay here after all that's happened. She's got a flight today. My cousin just texted me this morning about it."

"Back to Quest?" He couldn't believe it.

"Of course not! She doesn't have anything lined up, but she's leaving Gallant Lake. She even asked Cassie and Nick to take that dog she adopted."

She'd even made arrangements for the dog. And hadn't said a word to him.

Chapter Seventeen

Brittany was exhausted as she set her suitcase by the door. Between dealing with Blake's disappointment at her news after the meeting and packing and…you know…all the crying, there was no way for her to sleep last night. She wasn't sleepy, though. She was wired and felt like she was shaking, even though her hands looked steady. It was as if her body was trembling under her skin. Trying to tell her something?

Sure, she'd had doubts about her decisions. Lots of them. But there was no way she could stay until her situation with Nate was resolved. And she didn't see that happening. He'd left the meeting last night without speaking to her and hadn't reached out since.

Was he feeling guilty? Was he still angry that she hadn't told him everything before this week? Was he embarrassed? Did he hate the idea of condos at the resort, too? Did he just hate *change*, period? Did he hate her?

She stood at the window and watched Joey bounding around the yard chasing the crisp leaves coming down from the trees. The breeze sent them skittering across the lawn, Joey right behind them. She was going to miss that damn dog. She was going to miss the mountains and the lake and the town. Her friends. And Nate. A lump the size of a boulder rose in her throat. God, she was going to miss him so much. But he'd hurt her, and he'd left her. She squared her shoulders. So she'd have to find Brittany 3.0 somewhere else.

Her phone chirped. It was Ellie.

I'll be at the airport. You sure about all this?

Ellie had been asking that question for three days now. Instead of welcoming her big sister to stay with her in Raleigh, Ellie had continued to question the decision. Her phone buzzed again.

You're going to be on the sofa bed. Can you handle that?

She typed her answer angrily.

Do you not want me to come?

The answer was swift.

No I don't. I love you but you're being stupid.

They'd argued yesterday morning on the phone. Ellie kept saying that Brittany had sounded happier in Gallant Lake than she had in years. Ellie reminded her that she'd found a guy in Gallant Lake. That was true. And then she'd lost him.

It's only temporary, El. I need this right now. Please.

She didn't know where she was going to settle, but she couldn't stay here.

I have red velvet cupcakes and pinot noir waiting. We'll have a pajama party tonight.

Ellie's text was followed by a row of emojis blowing kisses and a GIF of a dog hugging another dog. Brittany was returning a line of the same emojis and a GIF of a laughing Minion when there was a knock on the door. She wasn't expecting her ride this early. Amanda had promised to pick her up around ten to catch the resort's shuttle to the city. Nick West said he'd return her rental car for her when he picked up Joey later. He and Cassie were taking the dog. Maybe they'd decided to come earlier. She braced herself to say goodbye to the stray who'd taken up residence in her heart so quickly.

She opened the door and froze. Nate stood on the steps. He was wearing the same clothes he'd worn yesterday. His hair was practically standing on end. She couldn't help herself—she reached out to smooth it. She'd barely touched him when she realized what she was doing. His eyes were as round as hers, and they stared at each other without saying a word. Finally, she managed to pull her hand back. She cleared her throat.

"Wh...what are you doing here?" Her voice had fled along with her composure.

Nate's gaze fell to the suitcases.

"You're really leaving." His voice was dull. Exhausted. Defeated.

"Yes."

"Don't."

"I have to."

"Britt..."

She spun away, unable to look into his warm brown eyes and deny him. He followed her into the house, but she kept her back to him. It was the only way to think clearly.

"I'm going to Raleigh to see my sister."

"You'll be back?" There was hope in his voice, but she couldn't mislead him.

"No, Nate. I can't stay here."

"Brittany, I'm so sorry." He was right behind her,

but he didn't touch her. "I was wrong. I was so freakin' wrong about everything. Louise and all her conspiracy theories got into my head and I… Then I saw you with Quest. And what you said about bilking people… I've been protecting this town for so damn long, Britt. I…" He pulled in a ragged breath. "I jumped to conclusions. I overreacted. I blew it. I was a jackass. I didn't mean to… Damn it, Brittany, I *love* you!"

His hand barely brushed her arm, but he may as well have touched her with a burning cigarette. She jerked away and turned, stabbing him in the chest with her finger.

"Don't you *dare* say that to me! You rejected my love, remember? Said you didn't want it?" Her voice rose. Joey started barking at the back door as if he'd heard her and wanted to help. She poked Nate again, sending him back a step.

"I'm so mad at you right now! You made me fall in love with this place, with these people, with *you*." She stabbed at him once more, but he held his ground this time. "You changed me, Nate. But you didn't change at all. You still care more about holding on to history than being happy. You're so afraid to let go of this family legacy of yours, as if you're the patron saint of Gallant Lake and that damn hardware store…"

"I'm selling the store."

Four words cut through her anger like a blade. She stared at him, trying to figure out what he was doing. She'd been in plenty of negotiations over the years, but this was a tactic she wasn't prepared for. Finally, she blurted out a reply.

"What?"

"I'm selling the store."

"Why?"

The mighty barracuda had been diminished to single-syllable responses. She couldn't understand what Nate was trying to do. Why on earth would he sell the store? He didn't answer, so she struggled to find more words.

"But...five generations...you love that place..."

"No." His voice was firm now. "It's a *place*. A building. A pile of stuff. What I love is *you*." He took her hands in his, and she didn't fight his touch this time. She was cautious, but also hopeful. She hadn't felt hopeful in a week. Nate gave her fingers a light squeeze. "You were right about me. I've never been a fan of change. But, Brittany, I'd give up *anything* for you. That hardware store won't keep me warm at night. It won't make me laugh about spiderwebs. It won't watch the moon rise on the water with me. It won't love me back."

"But..." This didn't make sense. He couldn't possibly mean it. "You're just saying that to get me to stay. You'd never really..."

"Not only will I list the store by the end of the day, but I'll also use the money to follow you anywhere. If you can't stay here, then I'll be where you are." He hesitated, his brows gathering. "Wait... That sounded creepy. What I mean is...if you *want* me to, I'll come with you. If you think you're competing with this town, then we'll start somewhere else. I'll give it all up, because that's how much I love you."

He looked so sincere. So intense. So full of love. "You actually mean it. You'd sell the hardware store... even leave Gallant Lake...for me?"

He cupped her face with his hands. Her conviction to avoid his touch evaporated, and her eyes closed as she breathed in the scent of him. He must have stepped closer, because she could almost feel his words against her skin.

"Don't you get it? I'd do *anything* for you. I love you so much, and I will never doubt you again. If you need me to move to Raleigh, then that's what I'll do. If you want me to find an office job, I'll do it. Suit and tie every day. For you."

Her laughter bubbled up, and she leaned her head forward until she felt his lips on her forehead, kissing her softly.

"I can't imagine you that way." And she didn't want to. "Gallant Lake is where you belong, Nate." He went still, waiting for her to clarify. "I think it might be where I belong, too." She sighed. "Where *we* belong. Damn it, I'm so confused..."

His hands rested on her shoulders, gently pushing her back enough that his dark eyes could meet hers. His were shining with emotion.

"Go to Raleigh, babe." Her breath caught at his words, but there was something in the way he said them, confident and tender, that kept her from protesting. His mouth slid into a slanted smile. "You've got the ticket. Go see your sister. Go do whatever you have to do, for however long it takes. Just promise me it's not a one-way trip." He searched her face. "Promise me you'll come back."

She nodded, and the motion made her gathering tears spill over. Her heart was pounding steadily in her chest, and she took her first deep, cleansing breath in days. He was giving her room to think. To plan. To *leave*. As long as she came back to him. And how could she not come back to the man she loved so much?

"I'll come back." She looked around them. "But the cabin may not be available."

His smile deepened. "I know a place where you can stay."

"My furniture is very modern. It won't fit in with your antiques very well…"

His arms slid around her waist, lightly tugging her against him. "If *we* can figure out how to fit together, I'm guessing our furniture will, too. Just like our dog and our cat figured out how to get along. It'll be…eclectic. Interesting." His lips brushed hers. "It'll be perfect."

He kissed her, slow and gentle at first, a kiss full of his remorse and gratitude and love. Then she pressed up on her toes and kissed him back, send-ing the kiss into more adventurous territory. Their heads turned and they both moaned as they clung to each other. They'd almost lost this, but…here it was. All the love. He nibbled her lip and kissed her again, deep and hard. She knew life would bring them more challenges as they fit their worlds together, but as long as they had love like this, they'd be just fine.

Epilogue

Three weeks later...

Brittany was ready to start pushing and shoving if people didn't get off this plane. Everyone seemed to have a huge overhead bag that refused to come out of the overhead bin, and they were taking their sweet time getting them down and moving forward. Didn't they know she had someone very special waiting for her in Gallant Lake, who she was practically jumping out of her skin to see? Nate said Blake Randall was sending the resort's limo to pick her up, and they'd be together in just a few hours.

She'd spent ten days with Ellie, talking and laughing and making plans. She'd spent so many years worrying about her baby sister that she hadn't realized Ellie was a grown woman now, with her own plans, her own friends and her own life. She was doing just fine and, in many ways, had more wisdom than Brittany did. Ellie was a planner like her sister, but without the panic factor thrown in. She was thoughtful. Practical. And a pretty damn special person. After spending the first few days catching up on talking and sleeping, they'd tackled Brittany's life over the next few days. She had no problem subletting her apartment in Tampa—that building had a waiting list of tenants. She contacted movers and set dates for everything to happen.

Then she'd flown to Tampa to pack up her clothes and label all her belongings. Some would be donated. Some of them the new tenant wanted to buy. And some she'd take with her. They were the ones she figured would be easiest to blend with Nate's things at the house and least likely to be damaged by cat's claws or stained by muddy paw prints.

She and Nate had talked every day. Often more than once. Sometimes for hours, especially at night, when they'd both be in bed and unable to sleep without hearing the other's voice. The distance was hard, but it had helped put things in perspective. They'd talked through her decision to not tell the whole story to Nate, which he understood. They were a new relationship, and then she'd felt trapped, as if it was too late. That was why she'd been frantically try-ing to fix it.

That wouldn't happen again. If something came up that one of them was uncomfortable with, they promised to talk it out, like they were doing on these late-night calls. Not to say there wouldn't be argu-ments ahead, but at least they had some ground rules.

She finally got off the plane and practically ran up the ramp to the terminal and toward the baggage claim. But JFK was a big place, and she was winded by the time she passed security and entered the main terminal. She forgot all about that and came to a dead halt the minute she saw him standing there. It was Nate. He was at the airport, standing right in front of her, a big grin on his face. As always, he was in jeans and plaid, with a tan Carhartt jacket. He'd told her it was getting chilly at the lake these days. He was holding up a hand-lettered sign. She was already rushing his way when she saw what it said.

Mrs. Thomas?

She stopped so quickly at the words that another passenger ran right into her, almost knocking her over. And still, she couldn't move. She read the sign again. And again. Then she looked up at his face. His dear, sweet, loving face. If she'd had any doubts about her decision to come back to Gallant Lake, they were gone now. She was home. He was her home.

She ran into his arms and kissed him so hard and

so long that several passersby called out to them to get a room. She and Nate didn't care. He swung her around, holding on as if he'd never let her go again. She was okay with that. She had no intention of leaving him. Both of their faces were damp with tears by the time he set her back on her feet. His smile seemed endless.

"New ground rule," he said, wiping his cheeks without any hint of embarrassment. "We don't ever spend this long apart again. Ever. Never. I don't care if I have to fold myself up in one of your suitcases. I'm not letting you leave me again."

She laughed, wiping her own face dry. "Agreed! Oh, Nate, it's so good to be home again."

He made a face, looking at the surging sea of humanity pressing around them, pushing toward the exits. Toward New York City.

"Not home yet, but soon. I couldn't wait for that limo to get back to Gallant Lake with you, so I hitched a ride."

"I'm not talking about a place, Nate Thomas. I'm talking about us being together. This…" She gestured between them, her hand brushing both their chests, connecting their hearts in the air. "This is home. You're my home."

His huge smile got wider yet. "Yeah? Good, 'cause I feel the same way, kitten." He waved the sign next to her. "Did you happen to notice…?"

"Pretty hard to miss, although I was more interested in seeing your face than some sign." She looked at it, then took it from him, reaching into her large leather bag. She pulled out her pen. A good Realtor always had pens on hand. Nate watched, forehead furrowed, as she made one slight adjustment. She crossed out the question mark, then handed it back to him. Now it simply read *Mrs. Thomas*. She arched one eyebrow. "Is that clear enough for you?"

"If there's one thing I've learned over the past few months—" he winked at her "—it's that making assumptions based on circumstantial evidence can get a person into some really deep llama dung, so I'm going to need to hear the word, lady."

"Of course it's yes." She kissed him. "It's an absolute yes!"

He swung her around again. They both ignored the muttering voices around them, even the one that called them "yokels." They didn't care about anything other than each other. But they couldn't leave that limo waiting all afternoon, so eventually they gathered all her luggage—Nate's eyes went wide, but he didn't say a word—and they loaded the car and headed home to Gallant Lake. They spent the ride wrapped up in each other. Nate told her about the antique bed he'd just had delivered, modified to hold queen-size bedding. She teased him about modifying an antique, but she was secretly impressed. That was something old Nate would never do. Maybe he'd needed to evolve into Nate 2.0 as badly as she'd needed to get to Brittany 3.0.

The limo dropped them at the hardware store, where Nate's van was parked. He pushed the door open and called out to Hank. "What do we say to pretty Brittany, buddy?"

Hank picked up his cue immediately and called out two words over and over.

"Marry me! Marry me! Marry me!"

Brittany started to laugh. "You're too late, pretty bird. I already said yes to your pal Nate." When she turned, she was shocked to see Nate on one knee. She'd figured that sign was a suggestion for something that would happen someday down the road. But clearly she'd assumed wrong. Because Nate was holding up a velvet box. He flipped it open to reveal a lovely gold ring with a heart-shaped diamond, with smaller stones on either side.

She smiled at him. "You didn't find that in a cobweb-filled old barn."

"Nope. It is vintage, but it was never touched by spiders, I promise." He took it out of the box. "Brittany Doyle, I know it's fast. I know we've made mistakes. I know we're complete opposites and we'll probably make more mistakes through the years. But please…" His expression grew serious. "Please say you'll marry me. Maybe not right away, but…"

"Yes! I already said yes, but now officially yes!" She tugged him to his feet and watched as he slid the ring on her finger. "I don't care when. I just want forever." ·

He pulled her in for a kiss. "I can definitely promise you that."

As his lips touched hers, Hank finished setting the mood for them, at the top of his lungs.

"Love you! Love you! Love you!"

* * * * *

Don't miss the other Gallant Lake Stories:

A Man You Can Trust
It Started at Christmas…
Her Homecoming Wish

Available now from Harlequin Special Edition!

And if you're looking for more opposites-attract romances, try these other great books:

Home for the Baby's Sake
by Christine Rimmer
The Last Man She Expected
by Michelle Major
Her Sweet Temptation
by Nina Crespo

Available now wherever Harlequin Special Edition books and ebooks are sold!

#2791 TEXAS PROUD
Long, Tall Texans • by Diana Palmer

Before he testifies in an important case, businessman Michael "Mikey" Fiore hides out in Jacobsville, Texas. On a rare night out, he crosses paths with softly beautiful Bernadette, who seems burdened with her own secrets. This doesn't stop him from wanting her, which endangers them both. Their bond grows into passion... until shocking truths surface.

#2792 THE COWBOY'S PROMISE
Montana Mavericks: What Happened to Beatrix?
by Teresa Southwick

Erica Abernathy comes back to Bronco after several years away. Everyone is stunned to discover she is pregnant. Why did she keep this a secret? And what will she do when she is courted by a cowboy she doesn't think wants a ready-made family?

#2793 HOME FOR THE BABY'S SAKE
The Bravos of Valentine Bay • by Christine Rimmer

Trying to give his son the best life he can, single dad Roman Marek has returned to his hometown to raise his baby son. But when he buys a local theater to convert into a hotel, he finds much more than he bargained for in Hailey Bravo, the theater's director.

#2794 SECRETS OF FOREVER
Forever, Texas • by Marie Ferrarella

When the longtime matriarch of Forever, Texas, needs a cardiac specialist, the whole community comes together to fly Dr. Neil Eastwood to the tiny town with a big heart—and he loses his own heart to a local pilot in the process!

#2795 FOUR CHRISTMAS MATCHMAKERS
Lockharts Lost & Found • by Cathy Gillen Thacker

Allison Meadows has got it all under control—her home, her job, her *life*—so taking care of four-year-old quadruplets can't be that hard. But Allison's perfect life is a facade and she has to stop the TV execs from finding out. A lie ended former pro athlete Cade Lockhart's career, and he won't lie for anyone...even when Allison's job is on the line. But can four adorable matchmakers create a Christmas miracle?

#2796 HER SWEET TEMPTATION
Tillbridge Stables • by Nina Crespo

After a long string of reckless choices ruined her life, Rina is determined to stay on the straight and narrow, but when a thrill-chasing stuntman literally bowls her over, she's finding it hard to resist the bad boy.

Mikey's fingers contracted. "Suppose I told you that the
hotel I own is actually a casino," he said slowly, "and it's
in Las Vegas?"

Bernie's eyes widened. "You own a casino in Las
Vegas?" she exclaimed. "Wow!"

He laughed, surprised at her easy acceptance. "I run it
legit, too," he added. "No fixes, no hidden switches, no
cheating. Drives the feds nuts, because they can't find
anything to pin on me there."

"The feds?" she asked.

He drew in a breath. "I told you, I'm a bad man." He
felt guilty about it, dirty. His fingers caressed hers as they

neared Graylings, the huge mansion where his cousin lived with the heir to the Grayling racehorse stables.

Her fingers curled trustingly around his. "And I told you that the past doesn't matter," she said stubbornly. Her heart was running wild. "Not at all. I don't care how bad you've been."

His own heart stopped and then ran away. His teeth clenched. "I don't even think you're real, Bernie," he whispered. "I think I dreamed you."

She flushed and smiled. "Thanks."

He glanced in the rearview mirror. "What I'd give for just five minutes alone with you right now," he said tautly. "Fat chance," he added as he noticed the sedan tailing casually behind them.

She felt all aglow inside. She wanted that, too. Maybe they could find a quiet place to be alone, even for just a few minutes. She wanted to kiss him until her mouth hurt.

Don't miss
Texas Proud *by Diana Palmer,*
available October 2020 wherever
Harlequin Special Edition books and ebooks are sold.

Harlequin.com

Get 4 FREE REWARDS!

We'll send you 2 FREE Books plus 2 FREE Mystery Gifts.

Harlequin Special Edition books relate to finding comfort and strength in the support of loved ones and enjoying the journey no matter what life throws your way.

FREE
Value Over
$20

YES! Please send me 2 FREE Harlequin Special Edition novels and my 2 FREE gifts (gifts are worth about $10 retail). After receiving them, if I don't wish to receive any more books, I can return the shipping statement marked "cancel." If I don't cancel, I will receive 6 brand-new novels every month and be billed just $4.99 per book in the U.S. or $5.74 per book in Canada. That's a savings of at least 12% off the cover price! It's quite a bargain! Shipping and handling is just 50¢ per book in the U.S. and $1.25 per book in Canada.* I understand that accepting the 2 free books and gifts places me under no obligation to buy anything. I can always return a shipment and cancel at any time. The free books and gifts are mine to keep no matter what I decide.

235/335 HDN GNMP

Name (please print)

Address   Apt. #

City   State/Province   Zip/Postal Code

Email: Please check this box ☐ if you would like to receive newsletters and promotional emails from Harlequin Enterprises ULC and its affiliates. You can unsubscribe anytime.

Mail to the **Reader Service:**
IN U.S.A.: P.O. Box 1341, Buffalo, NY 14240-8531
IN CANADA: P.O. Box 603, Fort Erie, Ontario L2A 5X3

Want to try 2 free books from another series? Call 1-800-873-8635 or visit www.ReaderService.com.

---

*Terms and prices subject to change without notice. Prices do not include sales taxes, which will be charged (if applicable) based on your state or country of residence. Canadian residents will be charged applicable taxes. Offer not valid in Quebec. This offer is limited to one order per household. Books received may not be as shown. Not valid for current subscribers to Harlequin Special Edition books. All orders subject to approval. Credit or debit balances in a customer's account(s) may be offset by any other outstanding balance owed by or to the customer. Please allow 4 to 6 weeks for delivery. Offer available while quantities last.

Your Privacy—Your information is being collected by Harlequin Enterprises ULC, operating as Reader Service. For a complete summary of the information we collect, how we use this information and to whom it is disclosed, please visit our privacy notice located at corporate.harlequin.com/privacy-notice. From time to time we may also exchange your personal information with reputable third parties. If you wish to opt out of this sharing of your personal information, please visit readerservice.com/consumerchoice or call 1-800-873-8635. **Notice to California Residents**—Under California law, you have specific rights to control and access your data. For more information on these rights and how to exercise them, visit corporate.harlequin.com/california-privacy.

HSE20R2

Love Harlequin romance?

DISCOVER.
Be the first to find out about promotions, news and exclusive content!

 Facebook.com/HarlequinBooks

Twitter.com/HarlequinBooks

Instagram.com/HarlequinBooks

Pinterest.com/HarlequinBooks

ReaderService.com

EXPLORE.
Sign up for the Harlequin e-newsletter and download a free book from any series at
TryHarlequin.com

CONNECT.
Join our Harlequin community to share your thoughts and connect with other romance readers!
Facebook.com/groups/HarlequinConnection

 **HARLEQUIN**